SCAVENGER ZOID

Paul Stewart is a highly regarded and award-winning author of books for young readers — everything from picture books to football stories, fantasy, sci-fi and horror. His first book was published in 1988 and he has since had over fifty titles published.

Chris Riddell is an accomplished artist and political cartoonist for the *Observer*. His books have won many awards, including the Kate Greenaway Medal, the Nestlé Children's Book Prize and the Red House Children's Book Award. *Goth Girl and the Ghost of a Mouse* won the Costa Children's Book Award in 2013.

Paul and Chris first met at their sons' nursery school and decided to work together (they can't remember why!). Since then their books have included the Blobheads series, The Edge Chronicles, the Muddle Earth books and the Far-Flung Adventures, which include *Fergus Crane*, Gold Smarties Prize Winner, *Corby Flood* and *Hugo Pepper*, both Silver Nestlé Prize Winners.

BIOSPHERE CROSS SECTION

- **A** Outer Hull
- **B** Mid Deck
- **C** Inner Core

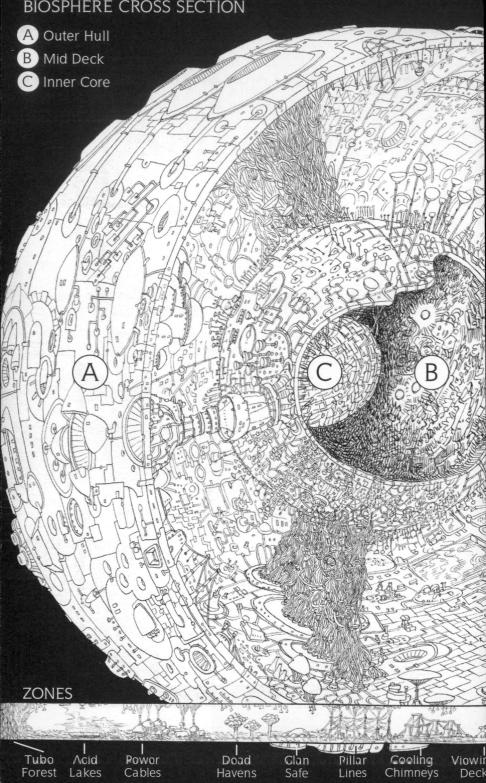

A

C

B

ZONES

Tubo
Forest

Acid
Lakes

Power
Cables

Dead
Havens

Clan
Safe

Pillar
Lines

Cooling
Chimneys

Viewing
Deck

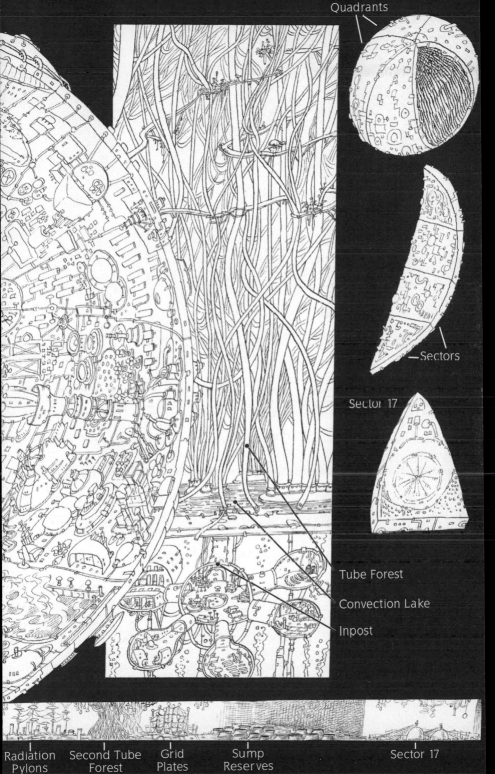

Quadrants

Sectors

Sector 17

Tube Forest

Convection Lake

Inpost

Radiation Pylons | Second Tube Forest | Grid Plates | Sump Reserves | Sector 17

MACMILLAN CHILDREN'S BOOKS

SCAVENGER
ZOID

PAUL STEWART

CHRIS RIDDELL

First published 2014 by Macmillan Children's Books

This edition published 2015 by Macmillan Children's Books
an imprint of Pan Macmillan
20 New Wharf Road, London N1 9RR
Associated companies throughout the world
www.panmacmillan.com

ISBN 978-1-4472-9995-0

1 3 5 7 9 8 6 4 2

A CIP catalogue record for this book is available from
the British Library.

Printed and bound by CPI Group (UK) Ltd, Croydon CR0 4YY

For Rick

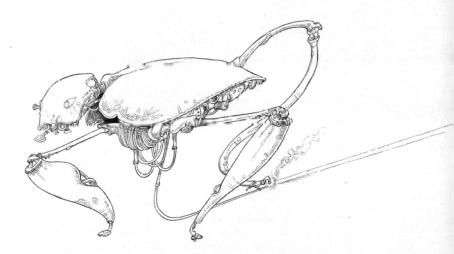

My name is York. I'm fourteen years old – leastways,
that's by the Half-Lifes' reckoning. Years don't mean
much in the Biosphere – nor months or days for that
matter. There are no days or nights here the way there
were on Earth.

I've seen pictures of Earth; the Earth we left behind
a thousand years ago. The Half-Lifes have shown me.
Trees, mountains, rivers; sunsets over deserts, moonrise
over the oceans . . . There's none of that here in the
Biosphere, only light from the hull lamps illuminating the
twists and tangles of the tube-forest that surrounds the
Inpost.

The Inpost is home. My home. It's the only home I've
ever known – or am ever likely to know. A run-down
mash-up of tech-sheds and mech-galleys hidden deep
beneath the tangle and scuzz of the tube-forest. OK,
it can smell of sweat and gunk-grease, and the holo-
simulations aren't up to much.

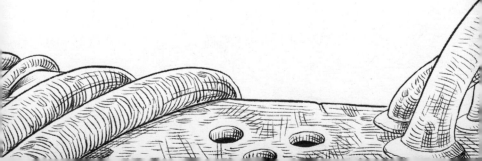

But it's safe. For now. At least, that's what Bronx says.

Bronx is the chief tech of the Inpost. He makes and mends. Scanner sights, stun-pulsers, cyber-implants – you name it, Bronx can construct it from zoid-junk. Everything it takes to keep us secure. All one hundred and twenty-six of us – not counting the two Half-Lifes, who aren't alive exactly, but aren't quite dead either. They're our ancestors, from the Launch Times, their consciousness downloaded into mind-tombs.

There are all sorts living in the Inpost, and everyone does their bit. Fixers, growers, watchers, salvagers, sanitizers, cook-techs, bev-servers . . . And then there's me. I'm a scavenger. There aren't that many of us. Not surprising really. Considering. We hunt zoids out in the tube-forest, kill them any way we can, then bring their

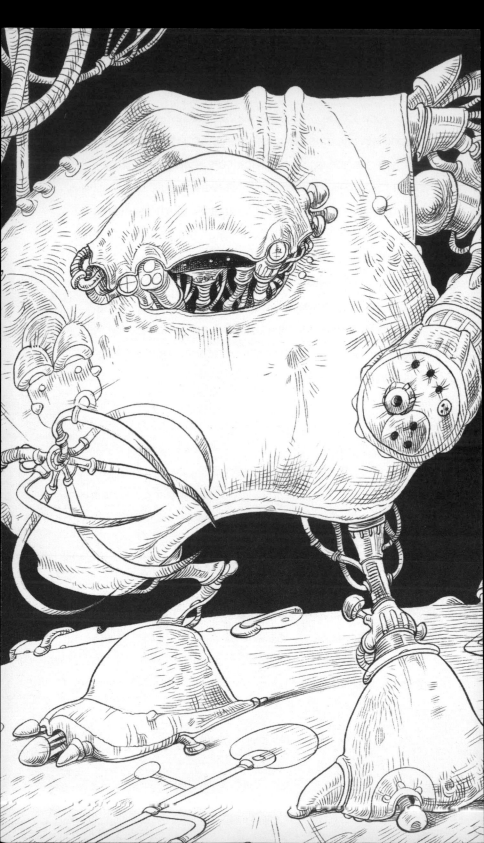

parts back to the Inpost for Bronx to use.

It's a dangerous job, but someone has to do it. Out in the tube-forest not even Bronx can keep you safe.

Just ask Dek, my best friend. I've known him as long as I can remember – ever since the nursery hub. We both lost our parents in the last big zoid attack. Not that either of us can remember. We were only babies back then.

That was when Bronx moved the Inpost from the turbine banks to Quadrant 4. Here, beneath the convection lakes in the middle of the tube-forest, we're hidden from even the most advanced zoids.

Not that they've given up looking.

You see, to zoids, humans are vermin, no different to the critters that infest the tube-forests. They're out to eradicate us from the Biosphere. To wipe us out. Maybe we're the only ones left. Maybe there are others. There's no way of knowing without leaving the tube-forest. And that's not an option. So we hide – and hit back any way we can.

It wasn't always this way. The Half-Lifes tell us about the Launch Times when robots served mankind, maintained the Biosphere and looked after our needs. Then something in the robots changed. The Half-Lifes can't tell us what. But the robots rebelled. They became killer zoids and took over.

They are the masters now, and we are their prey.

'To survive,' says Bronx, 'that is our mission. And in order to survive, we have to scavenge . . .'

Bleep.

The sound in my ear is soft and muffled. I keep my eyes shut and drift back to my dream . . .

I'm warm. I'm safe. I'm back at the Inpost, at the Counter, sharing a mug of bev with Dek. He's smiling

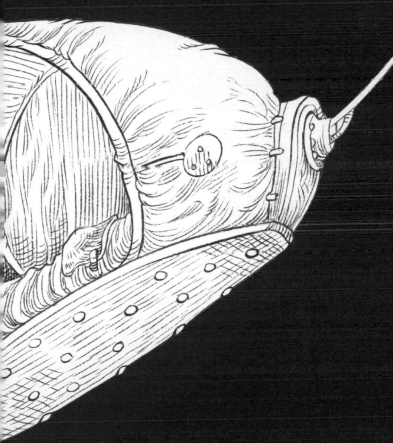

and teasing me because Lina, the girl who works at the trough-gardens, has just walked into the Circle.

It looks as though the whole of the Inpost has gathered, coming down tunnels from the sleep-bays and the work-hubs to crowd into the central space. Fixers from the clothing stores are swapping jokes with salvagers from the metal-shop. Sanitizers have abandoned their floor-polishers and hover-sweeps and are mingling with the growers in the hydroponic trough-gardens on the upper gallery, admiring the new harvest. A couple of watchers have left their monitoring stations and are playing soundscapes on music decks, while others, old and young, dance.

Lina comes towards me. I smile and hand her a mug of bev. No sweetener. Just how she likes it. Caliph, my pet skeeter, comes skittering through the legs of the crowd and jumps up onto my shoulder. He licks my face. Dek leans forward and ruffles the fur behind Caliph's ears, and I notice that instead of a cybernetic limb, his arm is real – and I'm happy because now we can go scavenging together, just like we used to before that killer zoid shot him up on the solder-walkway.

'You and me,' I say, 'we're a team.'

'Zoid whackers!' he says, and we raise our mugs.

Then I'm dancing, Lina on one side, Dek on the other, and the whole of the Inpost has joined in. Suddenly I hear Bronx's voice and, turning, I see him at the entrance to the tunnel that leads to the Half-Lifes' chamber.

'The Half-Lifes,' he says, and I can hear the excitement in his voice. He's thirty-seven, but has always looked older, worrying about us all. But not now. Now he looks younger than I've ever seen him look. Youthful almost. 'They know why the zoids rebelled. They know how we can defeat them. They know how humans can take back the Biosphere . . .'

Bleep.

I sit up, still drowsy. Rub my eyes. Tap my earpiece.

Bleep.

There's a zoid close by.

Bleep.

Suddenly I'm wide awake. I've been careless, not masking my heat-sig. And careless can mean dead, out here in the Open Halls.

I flick the coolant switch of my bodysuit and shiver as the flak-panels chill my skin. I hate sleeping cold, but I should've known better. I crawl out of the sleepcrib, climb to my feet and tap my wrist-scanner. The sleepcrib folds itself up – *flip-flap* – into the backcan strapped to my shoulders.

Bleep. Bleep.

If I'm lucky, it's a workzoid. A tangler or a sluicer. Neither of them have been programmed with much intelligence. On the other hand, it could be a killer.

Blip. Blip. Blip. Blip. Blip. Blip . . .

I move along the raised walkway, scanning the tube-forest through my recon-sight. I'm looking for the zoid's heat-sig.

And there it is.

A fuzz of orange surrounded by a rippled blue halo. It's a workzoid signature – and it's coming my way.

I catch a flash of movement. Then another. The zoid's laying cable. A tangler.

The bleeping becomes a single shrill note that whines in my ear. The zoid is directly beneath me. I brace myself. My heart's thumping. You only get one chance at a kill . . .

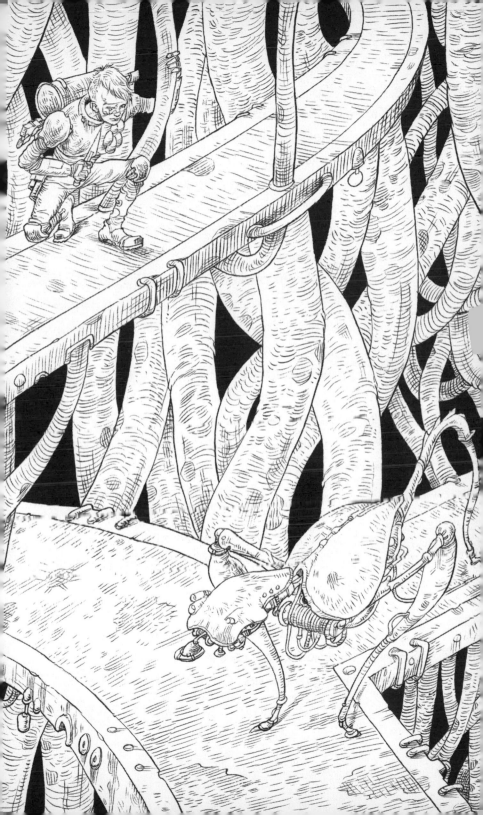

I drop.

My feet strike the curve of the tangler's back. The zoid keels over to one side, and I lash out with my cutter as the pair of us fall. The blade slices through tendons and bunched wires. I land on the floor of the gangway and roll clear – then look up.

The tangler's thrashing about, but it isn't going anywhere. I've severed one of its legs. A jet of blue-grey zoid-juice is gushing from the stump. Its head is swivelling from side to side, red sensors flashing. Loud clicks come from the perforated plate that covers its vocal cavity.

It's sounding an alarm.

I reach inside my flakcoat and pull out a gunkball. Flicking the detonator fuse, I press the soft putty against the smooth dome of the zoid's head, then step back.

The head explodes with a blinding white flash. Globules of molten metal and bubbling zoid-juice fizz off in all directions. The air stinks of fused circuitry.

I set to work.

The explosion has completely removed the tangler's head. Not that I've got any use for it. I'm after the good stuff. I rummage around in the mashed wires and dripping motherboard of the zoid's body and gouge out the command chip with the tip of my cutter. I strip out the zoid's central core, a shimmering backbone of prehensile urilium, and remove the alloy kneecaps from its legs.

My earpiece bleeps into life once more. High above me, I see the heat-sig of another zoid.

Hot swarf! It's blood red.

A killer.

I've been out in the tube-forest long enough. I backcan the tangler parts. They'll do very nicely. But as for taking on a killer zoid, that's just asking for trouble. It's time to leave.

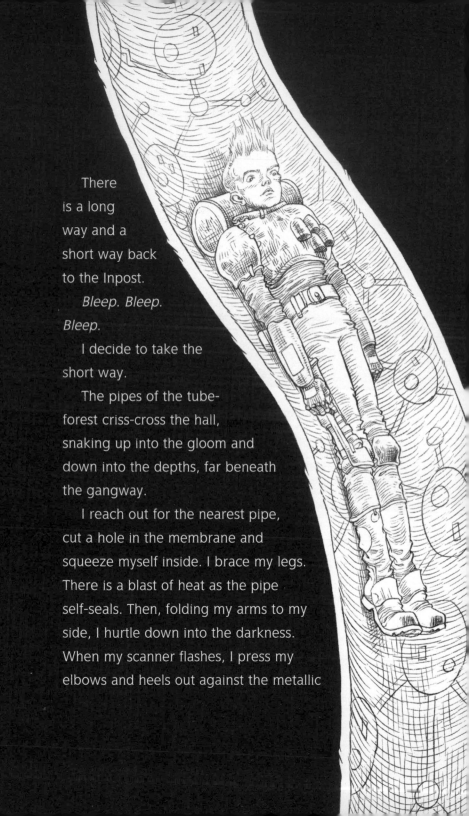

There
is a long
way and a
short way back
to the Inpost.

*Bleep. Bleep.
Bleep.*

I decide to take the
short way.

The pipes of the tube-
forest criss-cross the hall,
snaking up into the gloom and
down into the depths, far beneath
the gangway.

I reach out for the nearest pipe,
cut a hole in the membrane and
squeeze myself inside. I brace my legs.
There is a blast of heat as the pipe
self-seals. Then, folding my arms to my
side, I hurtle down into the darkness.
When my scanner flashes, I press my
elbows and heels out against the metallic

membrane of the pipe and slow my descent. I come to a halt. I cut through the tube wall a second time and clamber out.

The Inpost is just ahead, hidden deep down in the ventilation ducts. It's good to be back. On either side of me, the convection lakes crackle and fizz.

I begin to relax. Few zoids ever venture here. The power surges of the lakes mess with their workings.

'There y'are, York!'

I look up to see Bronx. He's got a boltdriver in his hand.

'Come quick,' he tells me. 'There's trouble with the Half-Lifes . . .'

'What kind of trouble?' I say.

In my dream Bronx had looked young. But this is the old Bronx. Careworn and worried.

'You'll see,' he says, and turns away.

He strides back along the gantry. I go with him.

A blue-white lightning bolt jags down and strikes the centre of one of the convection lakes. Steam billows up in a plume and the gantry is drenched with hot rain.

Bronx aims his wrist-scanner at the portal, and

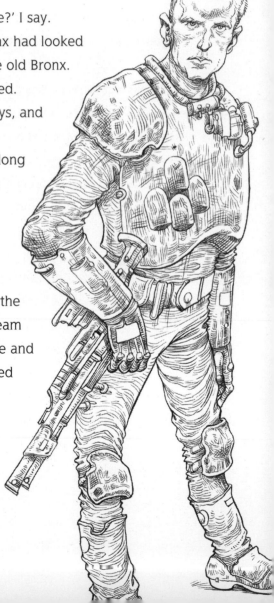

it slides open at our feet. The pair of us climb down the ladder inside. The rungs are hot, I notice, and twice vicious surges of static jolt through my body.

The second time it happens, the shock sets my backcan bleeping and flashing as it ejects my sleepcrib and stash of zoid parts and clatters to the floor. I fall after it and land in a heap.

Bronx turns to me, a hand outstretched. 'All right?' he says.

I nod. 'What *was* that?' I say.

'Power surge,' he says, helping me to my feet. 'It's been happening ever since you went out.'

He looks down at the zoid spine and the kneecaps I've scavenged, and nods appreciatively. 'Nice loot, York,' he says. 'Get it stowed and come with me.'

I reactivate the backcan, which scoops up my stuff, and send it scuttling off to my pod. Then I follow Bronx down the main tunnel to the Circle.

It's downtime, so the arc lights are off, but even so the Circle is busy. There are drinkers clustered at the Counter, some with bev and satzcoa; others on stronger brews. Menders are up late, repairing tattered shirts, suits and boots. Salvagers are working on zoid parts in the metal-shop, while growers on dark-shift are tending to the trough-gardens; pruning, harvesting, topping up the levels of biojuice.

As we walk past, one of the growers looks up. It's Lina. But she doesn't look at me.

'Greetwell, Bronx,' she says. The laser-shears she's holding illuminate her face. She looks concerned. 'So what do the Half-Lifes say?'

Bronx gives her his most reassuring smile. 'They say the Inpost is safe and the static will pass, Lina.'

He strides on towards the slip tunnel on the other side of the Circle. I follow close behind, uneasy about the lie he has just told. I sneak a glance back.

Lina is staring after us. Despite Bronx's smile and words, she's looking anything but reassured.

'Bronx . . . Wait!'

I turn to see my friend Dek coming towards us from the Counter, a mug of steaming bev held in his good hand.

'This new arm . . .' he begins. He raises his other hand, and I see how the metal fingers are flexing and bunching up, over and over. 'Can't seem to control it,' he says.

Bronx pauses and takes a brief look at Dek's arm. 'There's nothing wrong with it mechanically,' he says. 'And the flesh/metal surgery's been successful . . . It's this static,' he tells Dek. 'It seems to be spreading.'

I hear unfamiliar tension in his voice. I see sweat beading his brow, which he wipes away on the back of his sleeve.

'I'm working on controlling it, Dek,' Bronx tells him. 'But you're gonna have to give me some time . . .'

'Time.' Dek snorts. 'I'm not sure how much more of this I can take,' he says, his hand opening and closing faster than ever.

My friend Dek's one of the best scavengers we've got – or, rather, had. Ever since his arm got shot up, he's been out of action. Bronx's artificial limb was meant to solve all his problems.

'Whole arm's been acting up all downtime,' Dek continues. 'And it's getting worse,' he adds, his voice louder as Bronx turns on his heels and strides away from him. 'Have you spoken to the Half-Lifes?' he calls after him.

'That's just what he's about to do now,' I tell Dek as I hurry after Bronx, who's already halfway across the Circle.

Bronx and I take one of the slip tunnels. The lights seem dimmer than usual. A long spineback lets out a squeal and ripples off ahead of us, before scaling the wall on its sucker feet and disappearing into a narrow air vent.

Just then, there is the *scrit-scrat* of six tiny clawed feet as Caliph comes bounding up the tunnel to greet me. The skeeter scrambles excitedly over my chest and round my neck, then disappears into the pocket of my flakcoat.

We arrive at the Half-Lifes' chamber. Bronx enters, and I follow. The door slides shut behind us. And there, in front of us, stand the two Half-Lifes.

I look at the familiar faces that hover behind the domed casing of the mind-tombs. Something's definitely not right with them. Their images are flickering and flashing ominously.

The first Half-Life has cropped black hair, neatly brushed, and his firm, square jaw is clean-shaven. The second has long fair hair, flicked up at the ends. Her face is heart-shaped, her chin pointed. Laughter lines fan out from the corners of her hazel eyes.

Their faces are more familiar to me than my own. They flicker palely, their lips moving, while their voices, soft and level, whisper from hidden speakers.

Like I said, they're not alive exactly. But they're not dead either. According to Bronx, the Half-Lifes are what

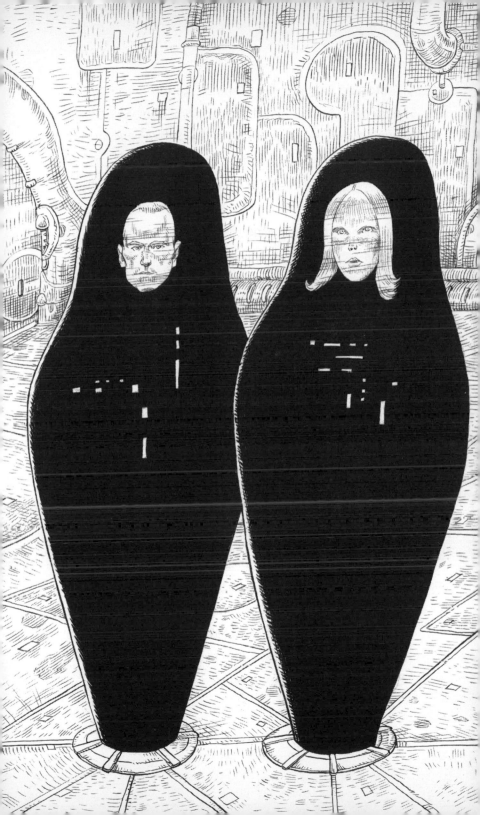

is left of the original crew of the Biosphere, that left Earth a thousand years or so ago. When their bodies aged and gave out, their minds were downloaded into these black data-towers: the mind-tombs.

We protect the Half-Lifes and they speak to us, their descendants.

They are speaking now.

'*The outer hull is no longer safe . . .*' Half-Life One hisses as the flickering grows more intense. '*Firewall breached . . . Scanning overrides . . .*'

'*Perimeter shell broken through,*' Half-Life Two announces, her voice partly obscured by a wave of buzzing white noise. '*Must seek lower levels . . . Return to the core . . .*'

The images suddenly jump and blur. The faces dissolve into lines and zigzags. They reappear briefly, only to disintegrate once more into a fuzz of static.

'Something bad's happening,' Bronx says.

He places his hands on first one of the black mind-tombs, then the other, as though this might heal them. But then both faces disappear.

'Are they . . . dead?' I breathe.

Before Bronx can answer, there is another sound, only this one is coming from somewhere outside. It is a low hum.

The sound of lasers slicing through metal.

'It's a zoid attack!' Bronx exclaims.

I stare at the two blank screens. 'Shouldn't we do something with the Half-Lifes?' I ask him. 'Hide them? Move them somewhere safe?'

'There's no point, York,' Bronx replies bleakly. 'They're just empty cases now. The Half-Lifes have gone.'

He turns and makes for the door. I follow him as he heads back down the slip tunnel.

The static is getting worse. The floor sparks and the air buzzes; tendrils of light crawl the walls.

As he approaches his pod, Bronx aims his scanner at the door. It opens in juddering fits and starts. The static again. He marches inside and crosses to his locker. The door opens and he reaches inside.

'Take this,' he says, passing me a pulser. 'And this. And this. And these . . .'

I shoulder the pulser, and the strapload of grenbolts he hands me. I holster the stunner and clip the firepick to my belt. Bronx has a pulser and grenbolt strap of his own, together with a pack of frack-grenades, which he loads into the pockets of his flakcoat. He reaches inside the locker again.

'Need more of these?' he asks.

I look at the open canister of gunkballs in his hand. Nod. Take half a dozen.

At that moment the Inpost sirens blare into life.

When we reach the Circle, the arc lights are on, but because of the power surges, they're flashing and sparking, throwing crazy shadows across the metal-shop and trough-gardens. In the dome above, a plume of smoke jets down from the glowing tip of a laser as it cuts through the ceiling. Spirals of swarf shower down like convection rain, and the air stinks of scorched metal. The laser comes full circle and a thick metal disc falls to the floor.

I stare up at the hole in the ceiling, recon-sight in place. I see a zoid heat-sig. Blood red.

Somehow a killer zoid has got past the convection lakes . . .

As I watch, the zoid drops down through the air. It's large and spheroid, striped copper and silver. It lands lightly on its two pneumatic legs. A dome-shaped head section tops a thick, articulated neck, and half a dozen or more arms spring from its body, tools and weapons appearing at the tip of each one. Lasers, blades, pulsers: the works.

The zoid must be an upgrade. I've never seen anything like it.

Beside me, Bronx's pulser bursts into life. A hail of molten grenbolts thuds into the zoid's body. They fizz for a moment, then explode in a series of blinding flashes, ripping the zoid apart from the inside. It's completely zilched. The smoking hulk pitches forward and crashes to the floor.

It couldn't have been easier.

But then a second killer appears at the hole in the ceiling. It's learned its lesson from the first zoid. Instead of dropping to the floor straight away, it extends one of its arms and sends a blinding line of laser bursts stuttering across the Circle towards us.

Bronx and I press ourselves against the opposite side of the slip tunnel as the air explodes all round us. Other Inposters are arriving, armed and in protective gear. They've responded to the sirens, and from the other tunnels around the Circle pulsers flash as they return fire. I catch sight of Dek, struggling to fire his pulser, and Lina, pulling the pin from a frack-grenade with her teeth, then throwing it.

The second killer drops to the floor, deflecting the grenade with a sweep of its arm and stepping smartly to one side. Then another killer drops to the floor beside it. Then another. And another. Five in all. They form a circle, keeping up a steady stream of laser fire directed at the tunnel entrances as they do so, forcing the Inposters to take cover.

I duck as laser bursts zing past my ear and bore holes in the tunnel wall behind me.

Then the killers each head towards a different tunnel, lasers blazing. More of them appear at the hole in the ceiling, brace, descend.

It's no good. We're being overpowered. Bronx and I fall back . . .

All at once, at the entrance to our tunnel, the *zing* of the zoid's laser fire falls still. There is silence for a moment. Then a new sound erupts. A high-pitched hissing.

I look up.

The zoid is sending out a stream of white light from deep within its body. It snakes through the air, hitting Bronx and enveloping him in a pulsating energy net.

Bronx jerks and spasms. His weapons clatter to the floor. The energy net tightens.

I watch, helpless, as the zoid hauls Bronx towards it. A panel at the front of its spherical body slides open and Bronx disappears inside. The panel slides shut.

I'm next. I realize I'm shaking.

I turn and run. Only when I reach the junction of the slip and exit tunnels, do I look back.

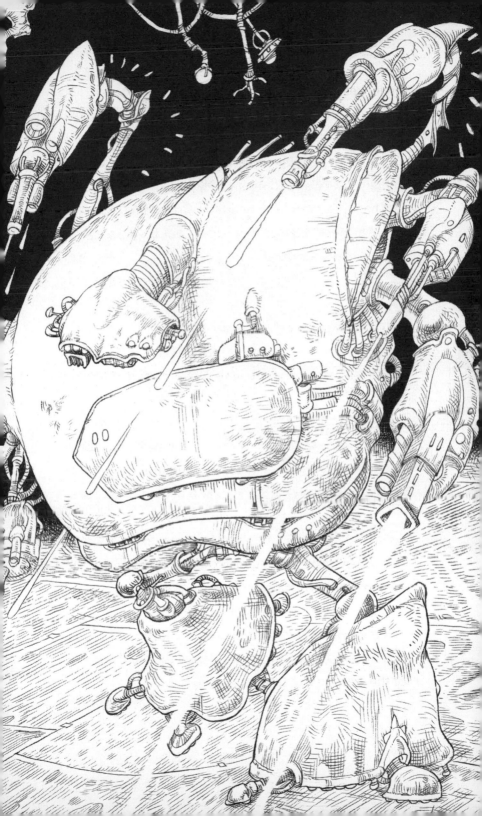

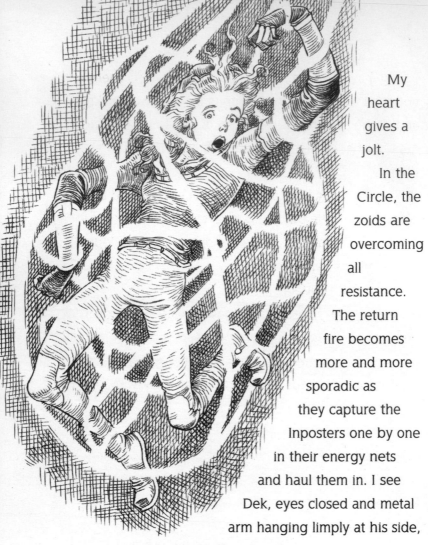

My
heart
gives a
jolt.

In the
Circle, the
zoids are
overcoming
all
resistance.
The return
fire becomes
more and more
sporadic as
they capture the
Inposters one by one
in their energy nets
and haul them in. I see
Dek, eyes closed and metal
arm hanging limply at his side,
disappear inside a zoid. Then I see Lina . . .

She's looking straight at me.

'Help me.' She mouths the words.

I raise my pulser. Take aim. But before I can fire,
the net snaps back and Lina disappears into the body
of the zoid.

My mind's racing. It's all happening so fast. There's nothing I can do. Not now. This is the only world I know and it's being torn apart in front of my eyes. I need to get out of here. Get my head together. Figure out what to do.

The arc lights flash on and off as I skid around a corner and hurtle down the main exit tunnel. I come to the ladder. I climb. Scan the portal – but it won't open.

My heart's hammering.

It. Will. Not. Open.

Reaching up, I press two gunkballs against the portal and flick the detonators. I drop back to the floor, crouch down and cover my head with my arms as best I can.

The explosion rips through the metal. My ears ring with the noise.

I climb the ladder a second time, navigating the jagged twists of metal, and leap out of the top of the pipe. I straighten up, gather myself, then hurtle off along the gantry, past the convection lakes and into the tube-forest beyond.

I don't know how long I run. It feels like forever. Finally, out of breath, I pause and scan the area behind me. Left, right. In front. Behind. There are no heat-sigs to be seen.

Not one.

No zoids. No humans.

A movement catches my eye and I look down to see Caliph's twitching nose sticking out of the pocket of my flakcoat.

'Caliph! I'd forgotten you were there!'

He looks up at me, and as I stroke his head all my emotions come surging up from inside me.

'It can't end like this. The zoids can't win. I won't give up on Bronx, Dek, Lina and the others . . . We've got to find them, Caliph. Rescue them. There's no one else left.'

I take the little critter out of my pocket and hold him close.

'You and me,' I whisper. 'Just you and me.'

5

I'm further from the Inpost than I've ever been before, and I don't like it. Not one little bit. It's still the tube-forest, but not a part that I'm familiar with.

We scavengers know the area around the convection lakes inside out – every twist, junction and switchback. The forest conceals and protects us. We've learned the best pipes to tube-surf down, the best walkways to hide on; where to set traps and where not to; which critters are harmless and which to avoid. And we're good at it – taking out workzoids quietly and efficiently, and staying hidden from the attentions of the killer zoids.

At least, that's what we thought. But we were wrong. They found us, and now there's no going back.

I have to find the Inposters. Swarf knows what those weird upgrade zoids are going to do to them. One thing's certain though: it won't be good.

But where have they been taken? And how much time do they have?

My thoughts are racing. I check my weapons. Button up my flakcoat. I feel cold sweat running down my back.

I'm going to have to venture even further from the Inpost . . .

Into the unknown.

Ducts, pipes and cables disappear into the distance in every direction. The power cables buzz and throb with electro-pulse and digital flux. The air ducts hum and moan.

Caliph lets out a soft mewling noise. He's hungry. And so am I.

'We'd best forage, boy,' I tell him, and I stroke his furry head.

I check my recon-sight and put in my earpiece. There's no trace of any heat-sigs, and we set off along the metal walkway deep into the tube-forest.

The critter calls get louder the deeper into the tangle of tubes we go, and the light begins to fade. Soon we're walking in near darkness.

All at once, the air crackles and there is a dazzling flash of light as a build-up of power is discharged from a cable up ahead. It illuminates the forest for an instant, then disappears.

I pull the pulser from my shoulder, load it with grenbolts and hold it before me. As I walk on, I point it into the shadows, my finger on the trigger. Caliph bares his teeth.

When the walkway splits, we head down a sloping

ramp. Then, keeping to the centre of a swaying cable-bridge, we cross a yawning void that is so deep I can't see the bottom. There is another dazzling flash of electric-blue light, and I catch sight of a swarm of pale-winged spotes darting and swooping beneath us.

We arrive at the far side of the bridge and pause. The pipes and tubes here are discoloured and corroded. I doubt a welder zoid has been this way in decades.

Mounds of thick dust line the rusty horizontal pipes, while others hiss with the pressurized steam that spurts out from small cracks, or drip with ice-cold water. And wherever there's moisture, the pipes are festooned with plants. There are trembling fern fronds. Swords of spikemoss. Broad, waxy-leafed succulents and ribbons of glowing air-kelp. And great clumps of dangling blue-grey grass that sway in the upcurrents of warm air.

These plants must have originated in seed banks, laboratories and green-zones somewhere in the Biosphere – places that have been wrecked by the zoids, their contents spilling out and taking root wherever they can. Weird thing is, they don't look like the Earth plants the Half-Lifes have shown us. It's as if they've mutated. And it's the same with the critters . . .

I hear a gruff bark close by. Raise my pulser.

Next thing, a huge critter, more than twice my size, emerges from the gloom. It's got long arms and short legs and a tail that looks to be three times as long as its body. Its movements are heavy and slow, and as it sways its head from side to side I see a single eye that stares out from behind strands of matted blue hair.

It moves overhead, using its long muscular arms and powerful tail to swing from pipe to pipe. A moment later, another appears. Then another, and another, until there's a whole colony of them sweeping slowly past.

I watch them enviously from the shadows below, wishing *I* could swing through the tube-forest with such ease.

When the last of them disappears into the darkness, and their barking calls have faded away, I scan the plants to find something I can eat. The scanner vibrates as its beam falls on a succulent covered in small spikes that is growing out of an air duct.

I tug the plant free, peel off the rough skin with my cutter, then slice off a piece and give it to Caliph, who seizes it in his front paws and sinks his teeth into the flesh. I take a bite myself. It tastes sour at first, then suddenly syrupy sweet, before filling my mouth with a tingling heat. I swallow. The weird sensation travels down my throat and hits my stomach, creating a deep, warm, throbbing glow.

I finish the succulent, then pull half a dozen more from the surrounding ducts. I peel them as well and

stow them in my backcan for later.

Caliph buries himself deep inside my flakcoat and I feel his body against my chest. Small and warm. Alive. Beating like a second heart.

'Now we need to find somewhere safe to sleep.'

Thirty minutes later, I stumble across the perfect place.

It's a tall, cylindrical tower that sprouts up from a twisted trunk of power cables, high above the surrounding walkways and tubing. I magnetize my kneepads and boot-hubs and start to scale the vertical sides of the tower. When I come to the first row of vents, I pause and peer inside.

I see a generator. It's humming and pulsing, but the fact that it's covered in a thick layer of dust tells me it hasn't been maintained recently.

Good. No danger of zoid work patrols.

There is no space inside the generator tower, but the flat roof at the top will do nicely. I climb up to it.

I pull out my sleepcrib and aim my wrist-scanner at it. It opens with the familiar *flip-flap* and secures itself to the roof. I crawl inside and lie down on my side. Caliph snuggles in against my chest.

I close my eyes and see Lina. And Bronx. And Dek. And all the others. Could I have done anything to help them? Or would I just have ended up in an energy net, being dragged into the guts of a killer zoid along with them?

I don't know. But I'm the only one left and I can't help feeling guilty. I have to find my friends, whatever it takes . . .

I must have drifted off to sleep, because suddenly I'm being woken. Caliph is chittering urgently. I'm face down. The sleepcrib is flapping about wildly as if something outside is trying to get in.

Whatever it is out there, it's big. Horribly big.

Caliph stays hidden down the front of my flakcoat, silent now and trembling. I feel around for my weapons. Pulser and grenbolts. Stunner.

I can hear wings beating outside.

With one hand gripping my loaded pulser I shift forward on my knees, pull the sleepcrib open and look outside. I am surrounded by huge ghostly shapes circling the tower on widespread wings.

There's a hundred of them. Maybe more than that.

Their small red eyes glow in the half-light. They have a curved bone ridge that juts back from the top of their skulls. As they flap round and round the tower, they suck in air through long, toothless snouts, causing the turbulence that is shaking the sleepcrib.

I climb out onto the roof of the tower and watch them glide silently around me in circles and figures of eight. They seem barely aware of my presence. Flying in endless loops, the ends of their snouts wide, they're intent only on sucking in air.

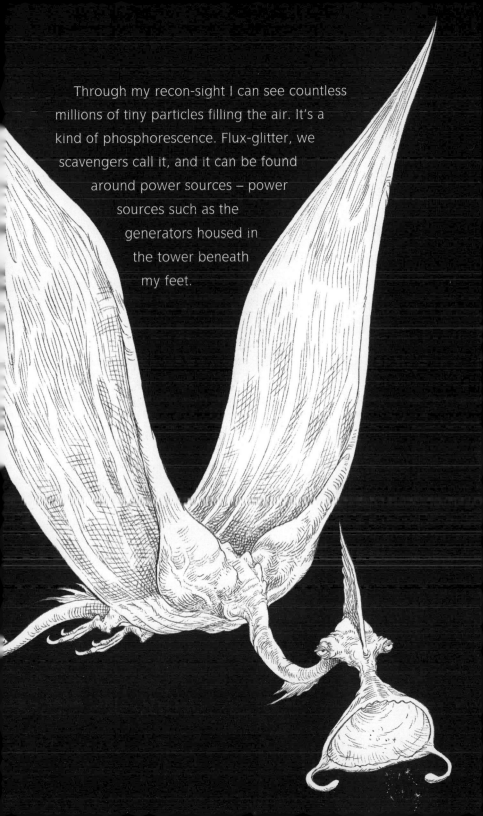

Through my recon-sight I can see countless millions of tiny particles filling the air. It's a kind of phosphorescence. Flux-glitter, we scavengers call it, and it can be found around power sources – power sources such as the generators housed in the tower beneath my feet.

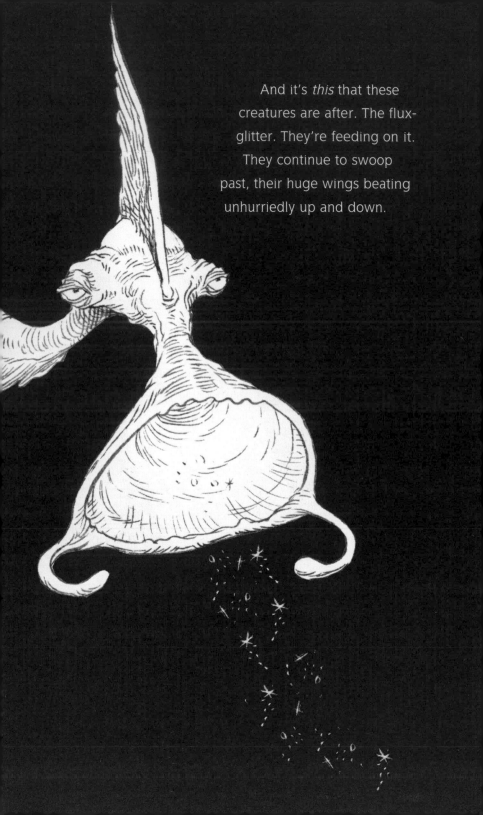

And it's *this* that these creatures are after. The flux-glitter. They're feeding on it. They continue to swoop past, their huge wings beating unhurriedly up and down.

Languid and regular. Mesmeric. As they swallow, the flux-glitter makes the end of their snout glow.

I make up a name. 'Glimmermouths.' I smile. It seems to fit.

Some of them come in to land. Soon there are as many on the flat top of the tower as there are in flight. And still they keep coming.

I lay my pulser aside, sit down and watch as they take it in turn to groom one another. They pay me no mind. The smell they give off – like hot wiring – grows more intense.

Caliph emerges from my flakcoat and sniffs at the air. He doesn't seem bothered by the glimmermouths. And nor am I. In fact, there's something oddly restful about being in the presence of this flock of gentle, flux-eating giants.

Far off in the distance, there is a blue-white flash as another power surge is discharged. For a moment the tube-forest is illuminated – pipes and helix-stacks draped with parasitic creepers and succulents that soften their hard edges.

It's vast. Back at the Inpost I hadn't realized just how vast.

I find myself wondering where the glimmermouths might have come from. How far they've travelled in their search for food.

Caliph takes hold of the cuff of my jacket and tugs.
I look down, stroke his little head. But the skeeter's
agitated. He begins to squeal. Fur on end. Teeth bared.

'What is it, boy?'

And then I see it.

Rising up into the air at the side of
the tower is some kind of tentacle.
It's long. Gelatinous. The width of the
pipes I tube-surf down.
The tentacle twitches and probes the air.
I need to get out of here. And fast.
Suddenly the glimmermouths spot the
tentacle and panic. They scrabble to their
feet and take to the air in a frenzy of
wing-flaps and glowing snouts that
concertina in and out.
The tentacle lunges,
making itself twice its
length. It seizes a
glimmermouth, coils
round it and plucks it
out of the air.
The glimmermouth
goes limp in the
tentacle's grip.

I drop to my knees, take aim and fire. The pulser jerks in my hand. The molten grenbolts explode as they thud into the tentacle, which uncoils, releasing its grip. The glimmermouth hurtles down through the air, one wing flapping, the other broken and useless.

I'm still watching it when there's a hard thump at my back that sends my pulser flying and me crashing to my knees. It's a second tentacle. It wraps itself around my chest and squeezes tight. Then tighter. Then so tight I can't breathe. I scratch and scrape with my hands at the smooth, cold, slimy skin. But it's no good.

Suddenly my stomach lurches as I'm yanked off the rooftop and whipped through the air. Next thing I know, I'm upside down and staring into a cavernous mouth directly below me.

Wet red flesh. Clacking fangs. A blast of warm fetid breath hits my face.

There're some gunkballs in the top pocket of my flakcoat. If I . . . can just . . . get to them . . .

My fingers slip. The tentacle tightens its grip. I can't breathe. The mouth comes closer.

My hand closes around a handful of the gunkballs. I pull out one, flick the detonator fuse, let it drop. Then another. And another. Five in all.

I count off the seconds.

Four . . . Three . . . Two . . . One . . .

All at once, there's a series of muffled thuds, followed by a wet, splattering explosion as the creature is blown apart.

And I'm dropping through the air, the ground coming up to meet me . . .

I land hard. I'm winded. The remains of the creature rain down. I close my eyes and cover my head with my arms as steaming blood, lumps of flesh and severed tentacles come thumping down around me.

Then everything falls still.

I open my eyes. Lying a little way off is a glimmermouth – the one I watched tumbling down out of the air. I climb slowly to my feet and walk over to it.

The critter's in a bad way. Its left wing is broken and it's having difficulty breathing. It stares at me, its red eyes filled with pain.

I can't let it suffer . . .

But I've lost my pulser, and my stunner, and I don't want to use my last remaining gunkballs. So I reach into my flakcoat and take out my cutter – only for Caliph to emerge from my pocket and leap down onto the shoulders of the stricken glimmermouth.

He looks back up at me, his body quivering.

'All right, all right,' I say, putting the cutter away. 'I'll see what I can do.'

The glimmermouth is lying half on its side, its wing twisted back. It doesn't look good. From the way it's wheezing I can tell it's in pain. Poor thing. I try to examine it as gently as I can.

I kneel down next to it and carefully turn it over. It moans softly. Then I run my scanner over its body. The bio-schematics tell me it's got three injuries.

Three of its ribs are broken, there's a gash at the top of its left leg that is deep but hasn't hit the main artery, and its left wing is broken.

It's not as bad as I thought.

I take out my medi-kit, then spray the glimmermouth's chest with quik-heal to numb the pain.

The glimmermouth exhales softly.

Caliph's sitting up on his hindquarters, so close to the glimmermouth that their snouts are all but touching. The glimmermouth doesn't seem to mind.

Next I lay pressure-gauze on its ribs and watch as the tensile material tightens around the chest. Bit of luck, the ribs should heal up fast.

I take a closer look at the leg. There's a lot of blood, but once I wipe that away the cut doesn't look too bad. I squirt a line of synth-skin over the wound and press the two sides together.

The glimmermouth reacts, but only with a slight flinch. It's braver than I would be.

'All done,' I tell it.

Once again the critter exhales softly. It's almost as though it understands me.

The wing is a bigger problem though. The wing bone has been shorn in two, and there's a splinter jutting out through the skin. It looks horribly painful.

There's no room for error here. I've got to set the bone *exactly* right. If I don't, then when it heals, the glimmermouth won't be able to fly. It'll just be stuck here on the ground at the base of the generator tower.

Until it dies.

My hands are shaking.

I clean the area around the break and spray it with the quik-heal. Then I take a hold of the wing with both hands. Caliph snuggles up close into the crook of the critter's neck and starts stroking its snout with one of its little paws.

I lean forward. I brace my arms.

'Three . . . two . . . one . . .'

I pull the bone outwards, then round. The

glimmermouth jerks and squirms as I push the two ends together.

I feel them click into place.

I lay a pressure-gauze pad on either side of the wing and watch as they mould themselves to the contour of the bone. Then I gently but firmly fold the wing back next to the other one.

'All we can do now is wait.'

Wait . . .

Thing is, I *can't* wait. I've got to find where the zoids have taken Bronx and Dek and Lina and the others. And this is all taking far too much time. Time they don't have . . .

The glimmermouth opens its eyes and stares up at me. I stroke the side of its head. Its snout glows as it makes a long mournful noise, deep and haunting. At first I think it must be in pain – but then I get it.

The critter is saying, 'Thank you'.

I sleep. When I wake up I scan the tube-forest. The dense, dark tangle of pipes and cables flickers with heat-sigs.

Critters not zoids.

I set off to forage food and water, leaving Caliph behind with the glimmermouth, who is sleeping.
The remains of the tentacled creature have attracted thousands of shiny purple insects. They swarm over the lumps of flesh in waves, devouring everything.

I leave them to it.

I spot several creatures feeding, but I leave them be. Live and let live.

Course, zoids are another thing entirely. They aren't alive. Zoids are the enemy. Zoids deserve everything they get. After all, they started this.

Back when the Biosphere was launched, robots ran the ship, protecting and serving the human crew. There was nothing they wouldn't do for us. But then something happened. Like I said, our Half-Lifes back at the Inpost couldn't – or wouldn't – tell us what. But the robots changed, re-engineered themselves without the aid of humans.

They changed their command protocols, their prime directives, even their appearance. Robots had been designed to look non-threatening. Sleek lines and curved shapes; some even had synth-skin coatings. But what they became, we humans no longer recognized as robots. Hard. Jagged. Deadly. And when they turned on us, we gave them a new name to match the sound of their weapon systems powering up.

Z-z-z-zoid . . .

I glance at my scanner again, to make sure. No zoids.

Further on, I find more of the succulents, harvest and stow them in my backcan, along with a whole load of plump mosses and some pale yellow vine-berries that my wrist-scanner confirms are edible. It's more than enough.

Water's no problem either. I come across a dripping coolant pipe. I fill my puri-flask and watch as the dark brown liquid turns clear.

Back at the tower, Caliph and I eat well.

The glimmermouth, however, is another matter. I need to press on, but I can't just abandon it. The thing is, it can't eat what we eat. It needs flux-glitter, and since it can't fly, it can't feed. I hope its injuries heal before it gets too weak.

Caliph's concerned about the critter too. He starts

squeaking insistently.

'I know it's hungry,' I say, 'but what can I do? There's no way I can get it enough flux-glitter.' I pause. 'Unless . . .'

I climb to my feet. I've had an idea. It's a long shot, but I've got nothing to lose.

'Stay here,' I tell Caliph.

With my kneepads and boot-hubs magnetized, I climb the side of the tower. I stop at the vents and peer in through the slats. The generator is humming, and through my recon-sight I can see clouds of flux-glitter all around it.

And, yes, just where I thought I'd seen it before, is a purple power cable coming out from the generator and connected to a network of external power lines.

I take the boltdriver from my backcan and quickly undo the vent-panel at the side of the tower. The panel slips from my grasp and clatters to the ground far below. Thrusting my arm inside the tower, I try to get hold of the cable.

But . . . it's . . . just . . . out . . . of . . . reach . . .

I climb up onto the vent-frame and push one leg through. The inside of the generator tower is cramped and grimy. Every surface I brush against is covered with a thick layer of greasy dust. I brace my boot against a rivet on the front of the generator and stretch forward.

My hand closes around the end of the cable. I grip it, try to turn it. It's slippery with the grease, but I feel a slight movement. Squeezing as tight as I can, I push and turn. All of a sudden there's a soft click as the end of the cable disengages, and the whole lot comes away in my hand.

The cable is like a thick length of hose. One end is still connected to the generator and, once I adjust my recon-sight, I see the flux-glitter gushing out from the other end like water. I take care. If I accidentally touched this end, the shock would burn me to a crisp in an instant.

Slowly, gingerly, I ease myself out of the generator space. Then, holding the cable away from me, I climb back down the tower. Caliph takes one look at the cable and darts away, hissing. The glimmermouth, on the other hand, is spellbound, its red eyes fixed on the end of the cable and the swirling mass of flux-glitter it can see pouring from it.

'Hungry?' I say.

Holding the cable in both hands, I reach forward until

the end is almost touching the glimmermouth's snout. It starts feeding, sucking in the dense cloud of flux-glitter and gulping it down. Soon it isn't only the tip of its snout that's glowing, it's the critter's entire body.

And as it eats, it gets stronger. The change is amazing. It's turning a rich golden colour, while its eyes, which had grown dull, gleam ruby red. It flexes its shoulders. Its chest expands. It pulls itself up onto its hind legs.

Caliph squeaks with encouragement as, wobbly but upright, the great glimmermouth steadies itself. Its wings begin to stir.

'You can do it,' I whisper.

It lifts its head, then slowly raises its wings.

Tentatively at first, but with growing confidence, the glimmermouth starts to flap its wings. Back and forward. Up and down. I can feel the air move. Caliph dances about excitedly.

Then the creature turns away. Its eyes are wide. Its snout twitches.

It must be wondering where the rest of the flock has got to.

Its raised wings tremble. It braces its legs and launches itself off the ground. With long, powerful wingbeats the magnificent glimmermouth soars up into the air and disappears into the gloomy forest of pipes and tubes.

I stare after it. There's a lump in my throat. To think that it almost died. I'm happy that I was able to save its life, and even happier that it is able to fly.

And yet, despite that, I'm sorry to see it go. I'd grown attached to the critter.

Caliph had too. I turn and hunker down next to him. Pull him towards me; stroke his head, his chin, his back.

'We'd best get going,' I tell him. 'Before . . .'

I look up. See movement. The glimmermouth. It's coming back!

Caliph leaps away from me. And as the critter comes down to land, he jumps up and perches on its shoulders. The glimmermouth turns, fixes me with its red eyes.

And I understand. 'You're sure . . . ?'

I scramble up onto the glimmermouth's back and grasp hold of its shoulders. On either side of me, the great wings begin to flap. Then, with a lurch, the glimmermouth launches itself back into the air.

We dip for a moment and I'm frightened I must be too heavy. But then the powerful wings start beating rhythmically, powerfully, and we soar high. I glance across at Caliph, then up ahead. The tube-forest seems to stretch on forever. But now, up here, high above the tangled chaos, I'm able to think clearly at last – think like a scavenger.

And I smile as a plan starts to form . . .

Flying. I'm *flying*!

The nearest I've come before is tube-surfing. This is different.

This is amazing!

The warm air in my face – buffeting my skin, ruffling my hair. The feel of being airborne, from the gentle tilt and sway as the glimmermouth glides and wheels, to the heaving stomach-churn I get each time it goes into a dive or soars up high.

And the most amazing thing of all: it's so fast. The ground rushing past in a multicoloured blur below me; the light panels speeding by above my head; flux towers and power pylons looming up on all sides as we sweep between them.

All at once, the landscape below changes. This is it. The end of the tube-forest. A great chequered plain spreads off into the distance. It's like a circuit board, but on a vast scale.

The glimmermouth cranes its neck around and looks back at me. Then it turns away again. Holding its

shoulders, I tighten my grip with my right hand – and the glimmermouth glides smoothly to the right. I tighten my left hand. It glides to the left. I lean forward, it flies lower. I lean back, it flies up.

Not only am I flying on the back of the glimmermouth, but it's letting me control its flight.

I keep my earpiece pressed into my ear and my recon-sight lowered. I concentrate. I listen. I keep my eyes peeled.

Suddenly my earpiece bleeps an alarm. I look round. The bleeping gets louder. Out of the corner of my eye I catch sight of a heat-sig directly below. Blood red. It's just what I'm looking for.

A killer zoid with a memory module.

I lean forward. I pull the last two gunkballs from my pocket as we swoop down towards the zoid. The zoid looks up . . .

It's big and mean-looking. Definitely a killer, though not the most recent upgrade. There's no compartment in its chest, which means that this one hasn't been designed to abduct humans like the ones that attacked the Inpost.

Just to kill them.

The killer zoid raises one arm and fires.

'Hot swarf!' I mutter as a blade of laser fire just misses me.

I flick the detonator switches on the gunkballs. The

glimmermouth wheels around directly above the zoid. I reach down and slap the gunkballs onto the zoid's dome-shaped head.

The glimmermouth soars up into the air.

The explosion is muted – a kind of muffled *flupp*. The zoid's head explodes. The flashing lights go out. The weapon-arms go limp and it keels over.

I've got a short time before other killer zoids arrive on the scene to see what's happened. A short time to get the info I need.

The glimmermouth lands and I climb from its back. I look down at the zilched zoid lying on its front at my

feet. Its head's been shot to pieces, but the body – which is where the important stuff's kept – is still intact. I scan the zoid's bolts. I remove the back panel.

Behind the smooth cover are the motherboard, the input/outport docks . . . and a self-destruct mechanism.

I groan. It's been activated. I've got even less time than I thought.

I inspect the motherboard – identify the weapons centre, the movement hub . . . And there it is, the memory module. I press my scanner against it and see the memory download.

Suddenly my head fills with the sound of bleeps coming from my earpiece. I look up. Through my recon-sight I see half a dozen blood-red heat-sigs heading across the plain, straight for us.

I grab the scanner and jump onto the glimmermouth's back, Caliph clinging to my flakcoat. We soar up into the air. Just in time.

There's a colossal explosion as the zoid self-destructs.

We're buffeted by the shock waves of the blast. The glimmermouth rolls and tumbles in the air, forcing me to cling to its back for dear life. But when the creature rights itself, I smile.

The bleeping in my ear has stopped. The other zoids must have made it to the killer, and the explosion has destroyed them. Every single one.

Below me, the end of the circuit-board plains approaches. I lean forward and scrutinize the view ahead through my recon-sight.

There are six vast rectangular pools laid out in a long line, light gleaming on the surface of the water. Except it isn't water.

It's acid.

The air's got this pungent odour to it that's bringing tears to my eyes. Caliph can

smell it too. His nose is twitching and he's crouched down, rubbing his paws up and down his face. The glimmermouth's snout has irised shut.

I know this place. Leastways, I've heard about it.

The Acid Lakes Sector. The edge of our world. No one from the Inpost has ever ventured beyond here. Not even Bronx. We've always kept to the tangle and twist of the tube-forest – where there's food and water and places to hide.

Not like these lakes. They give off fumes so strong, you get too close and they'll melt your eyeballs and dissolve your lungs.

The Half-Lifes call them 'digesters'. In the Launch Times, all waste matter – animal, vegetable or mineral – was gathered up by refuse-robots and deposited in the acid, where it would dissolve, while duct pipes criss-crossing the lakes' surface sucked up the fumes and recycled them as fuel and biosoil.

When the Rebellion began, the refuse-robots upgraded themselves and became zoids, along with the domestic robots, recreation robots, gardening robots – in fact, any robots that had been designed to directly serve humans. After the Rebellion, the zoids turned the duct pipes off and left a thick, poisonous scum hovering over the surface of the lakes.

The fumes didn't bother *them*. And it's us humans

who are the waste matter now.

'Come on,' I tell the glimmermouth, leaning right back and squeezing its shoulder tightly with my left hand.

The glimmermouth flaps hard and soars up high, then wheels around in a broad arc. Below me, all trace of life has vanished. Nothing could survive in this corrosive environment.

We skirt the edge of the line of lakes. Wisps of noxious steam dance on the surface of the acid, but we're too high for the fumes to bother us and the glimmermouth flies on with strong, steady wingbeats.

The acid lakes fall away behind us. Ahead lies a new, unfamiliar landscape. The hull lights high overhead are dimmer. Instead, the light comes from domes that mushroom up from the ground and glow. Power cables sprout from all directions, connecting the domes to each other in a vast network. Pulses of light pass along the cables in glittering streams, and there is the low, pervasive hum of cooling systems, though the air feels hot and clammy.

Down below, I spot a huge, low structure through my recon-sight. It has no static and there are no discernible heat-sigs. It looks like some kind of hangar. I bring the glimmermouth down to land on the roof.

Caliph lets out a little squeak and jumps down from the creature's back. I do the same.

I take the opportunity to check the memory download from the killer zoid.

'Play zoid download,' I tell my scanner.

At first the screen is blank. Then images appear and the action unfolds in reverse. I'm watching the zoid's eye-cam.

There's an explosion. Then I see myself plucking the gunkballs from the zoid's head, flying backwards on the back of the glimmermouth, Caliph beside me, the three of us shrinking to a small dot. The focus of attention jumps to a forest of receding tubes and pipes.

This isn't what I'm looking for.

'Search central memory bank,' I tell the scanner.

It flashes up tiny screens – hundreds of them – from throughout the sector. They're the eye-cam downloads of the various zoids. I see pipe clearance, solder repairs, cable laying . . .

'Search red signatures only,' I say.

The screen freezes as the scanner narrows its search.

Then ten red eye-cams appear. I scroll down them, then stop. My stomach gives a lurch.

'Play,' I tell the scanner.

I'm looking through the eye-cam of one of the killer zoids that attacked the Inpost.

There are the Inposters. Dozens of them. Familiar faces. Lev, who serves satzcoa and bev at the Counter;

Sala the gardener and her friends, Effi and Spalding;
Misha the watchman, who monitors the perimeter
screens; Tara, Delaware, Fitch . . .

They're inside some vast building I don't recognize.
Most of them are penned up together; seated, standing,
pacing back and forth. The force field that imprisons
them glows a silver-red. Among them I see Bronx. And
Dek, whose arm doesn't seem to be bothering him now.
And Lina.

The three of them are standing at the edge of the
pen, looking at something. Dek's comforting Lina, whose
face is crumpled up, distraught.

I enlarge the view.

There's a row of steel chairs over by the far wall.
An old man has been secured to the nearest one, his
wrists and ankles secured by steel rings. He's got a shiny
helmet on his head, and from the bushy white beard I
recognize him at once.

It's Gaffer Jed. Lina's grandfather. A kind old man. Friendly. Harmless. Always telling stories to the kids of the Inpost – including me, when I was younger. The Half-Lifes had the facts, but it was Gaffer Jed who made the past come alive, with his stories of blue Earth skies and billowing clouds of white water vapour, and forests of mighty plants called trees; stories told to him by his gaffer, and his gaffer before him, all the way back to the Launch Times . . .

The killer zoid beside him is holding a laser saw and a probe.

I look away. There's a pain in my chest, as if I've been punched. I've got to do something. I've got to help them.

But where are they?

The scanner identifies the place as being in a zoid-only zone. Sector 17. I didn't even know there was a Sector 17.

But I'm going to have to find it.

Suddenly my earpiece starts bleeping again. I curse out loud. Looking down from the edge of the roof I see the heat-sig of a single zoid approaching. Pale yellow.

Moments later it comes into view.

I've never seen anything like it. It's squat and round.
It has stubby legs and two extendable arms that have
pincers at the ends. And a face. Two glowing eyes; a
mouth that's set in a kind of half-smile.

This was considered reassuring back when the
Biosphere was run by robots who worked for humans.
So this must be an ancient robot.

As I watch, a portal opens in the building below me
and the ancient robot waddles inside. The portal slides
shut with a hiss. Leaving Caliph with the glimmermouth,
I magnetize my boot-hubs and body armour and climb
down from the roof.

The portal has a rudimentary movement sensor. No
security. Whatever's inside can't be worth protecting.
The portal slides open again.

I take out my cutter and step into the darkness inside.

Ahead of me, the robot pauses. Its head swivels, its
eyes flash. A low hum comes from its smiling mouth – but
before it can say a word I press my scanner to the side of
its head and zap its control centre with a pulse of energy.

I'm guessing a robot this simple has no deflectors.

Sure enough, it slumps forward. If only zoids were this easy to deal with.

I open up its head. The motherboard's much simpler than the ones I usually come across when I'm scavenging. It's got a small memory – just enough to enable it to perform simple tasks. Locating the interface unit, I reconfigure it with my own personal identification data. Old tech. It'll respond to my commands now.

Or should do.

I close the head. Step back. Reboot it with my scanner.

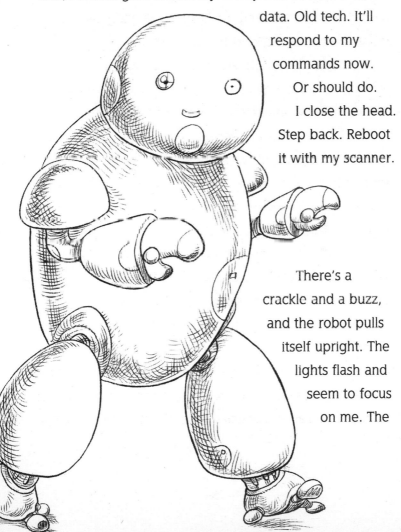

There's a crackle and a buzz, and the robot pulls itself upright. The lights flash and seem to focus on me. The smiling mouth speaks. 'Greetings, crew-member York. My name is Ralph. How may I serve you?'

The voice is calm, soft, reassuring. These ancient robots were programmed not to harm humans, nor, by inaction, to allow a human to come to harm.

'Ralph?'

'Robotic Assist-Level Personal Help, sir. How may I serve you?'

I look around. 'Well, Ralph, you can start by telling me what this place is.'

'This is the Central Robot Hub, sir,' it says, and raises one arm. A line of light panels comes on in the ceiling at the far side of the building. 'You are most welcome to inspect, crew-member York, sir.'

I smile to myself. No one's ever been this polite to me before.

Now I can see better, the place looks even bigger than it did from the outside. There are racks of shelves lining the wall opposite. Most of them are empty, though some are subdivided into stacks of stock-lockers, each one embossed with a glowing light that details its contents.

Gradient Sockets 54/i. Terminal Drives c14–c21. Helix Springs . . .

I aim my scanner at one of the lockers. It's labelled *Input Processors – Delta-Mode/iv* and slides open to

reveal a mass of silver components I can't identify. Inside
the next locker – marked *Tube De-Blockers: Max Str* – is
something I do recognize.

Gunkballs.

I take a dozen of them and put them in my backcan.
Then a dozen more. Ralph makes no move to stop me.

Behind me, more of the overhead panels come on.
I turn to see the entire hangar bathed in light – and an
army of inert robots standing in rows, their shadows
pooled around their feet.

I must have gasped with surprise because Ralph says,
'I did not catch that, sir.'

I shake my head. 'A lot of zoids . . . I mean, robots
here,' I mutter.

'The Robot Hub houses three hundred and sixty
complete refits, sir. Twelve models. Thirty units per
model—'

'Show me.'

Ralph waddles to the end
of the line. I step forward
and inspect the troops. A
dumpy blank-faced robot
stands before us. It has
a barrel-shaped body
and hover-jets instead
of legs. Behind it, a line

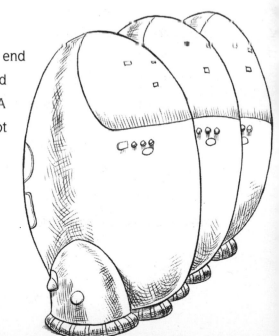

of identical-looking robots stretches far back into the distance.

'This is a refuse-robot, sir,' Ralph announces. It moves to the next column, its legs swivelling round, but head remaining forward. 'This is a domestic-robot, sir.' It moves again. 'This is a leisure-robot . . .'

I'm intrigued by these ancient robots. I guess they must have been in storage when the others changed into zoids.

I move down one of the lines, then cut through the ranks at an angle. I check my recon-sight. There's Ralph, and me, and the pulsing heat-sigs of Caliph and the glimmermouth up on the roof above, but no sign of any zoids.

'This is a gardener-robot,' Ralph is saying.

I pause. It's short and angular, and there's an amiable blankness to its face. It has three legs and two arms, all five limbs extendable. One arm has a hose attachment for watering. The pliers-like hand is holding laser-shears, which I take.

'If you require an energy source to recharge any tools, sir, I can take you to—'

I pull the trigger. The laser-shears hiss and dazzle.

'They seem fine,' I say, and holster them. I pat my stomach. 'What I do require, Ralph, is a *food* source.'

'A food source. Of course, sir.'

Ralph bustles through a couple more rows before coming to a halt in front of the most human-looking robots I've ever seen. They've got arms and legs, and hands and feet, all of them jointed. They've got heads shaped like human heads, with ears and noses and mouths. And eyes that look like real eyes.

It's incredible! Nothing in Bronx's cybernetic workshop comes close.

There are only three of these humanoid robots, not thirty. Ralph activates them, and they bleep and nod into action.

'Butler-robot at your service,' one of them says.

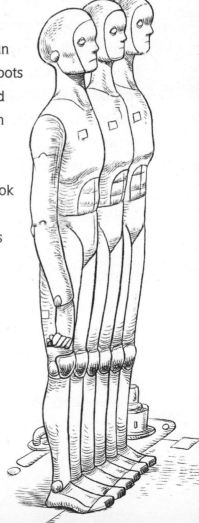

'At your service, crew-member York, *sir*,' Ralph corrects it.

'Butler-robot at your service, crew-member York, sir. What is your desire?'

'My desire is for a slap-up meal,' I tell it. I'm enjoying this.

'And will sir be dining alone?'

I look around me. Shrug. 'Looks like it.'

'Dinner for one,' the butler-robot announces.

All three butler-robots burst into feverish activity. They scurry and flap. They come and go. A tray transforms itself into a chair; a second into a table. Eating implements are placed at precise angles around an ancient plate, bowl and visiglass beaker.

One of the butler-robots pulls the chair back. 'If you'd care to sit down, sir.'

I do so. I can't help grinning. If this is how it was, then humans certainly lived the good life back in the Launch Times . . .

A second butler unrolls a square of cloth and tucks it in at my front. A third appears with a visiglass container; a fourth with a silver tray with a domed lid.

I prepare myself for a feast. It'll be the first proper meal I've had since the Inpost was ransacked. My stomach gurgles.

'Would sir care to taste the wine?'

I nod. The container is tipped up, but nothing pours into the beaker. I look at the butler-robot. It looks back at me with amiable anticipation on its face. I nod again. It tips the bottle further, as though filling the glass to the top.

But there's nothing there.

The robot with the silver tray steps forward. 'Be careful, sir, it could be hot,' it says, as it lifts the domed lid and holds out the tray.

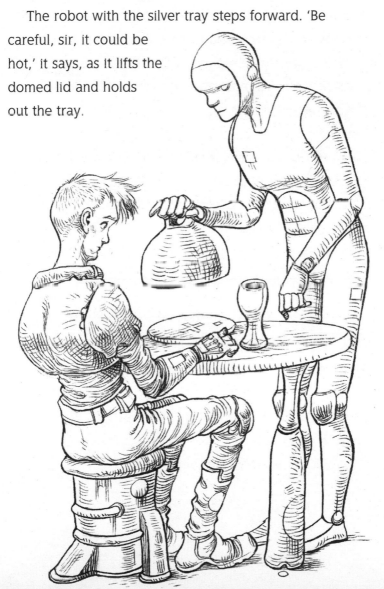

It is as empty as the visiglass container.

The robots are going through the motions. There obviously hasn't been food or drink to serve for hundreds of years.

I push my chair back and climb to my feet.

'I trust you enjoyed your meal, sir,' says Ralph, and if it hears me snort this time, it does not respond. 'Is there anything else I can help you with at this time, sir?'

'Yes,' I say. 'I need to get to Sector 17.'

'Sector 17,' Ralph repeats. There is a brief pause. 'I can navigate you to that exact position, sir. If that is your desire.'

'It is,' I tell it. Though even the thought of the place fills me with horror.

As we emerge from the hangar, the sound of chattering breaks into my thoughts, and Caliph comes bounding towards me. His nose is twitching and his tail's all bushed up.

High above us, wheeling around in slow circles, is a great flock of glimmermouths. The air is full of booming hooting calls. Gliding past the glowing domes, they're sucking up the sparkling clouds of flux-glitter through those long snouts of theirs.

Only one glimmermouth is not airborne. *My* glimmermouth.

It's still perched up at the top of the hangar where I left it, looking back and forward between the flock and me. Then our gazes lock. Its small red eyes narrow.

It glides down to land at my side. I reach out and stroke its neck. It stares up at the other glimmermouths again, and I recognize the yearning in its eyes. Then it turns to me, its head cocked.

'Thank you,' I say simply, swallowing away the lump

in my throat. I gesture upward with my arms. 'Now go. *Go!*'

The glimmermouth stares at me a moment longer, then abruptly turns away. It trots forward, awkwardly, its wings raised and keeling from side to side. There's a *slap-slap* sound as it flaps down hard. It launches itself from the ground, soars high and joins the rest of the flock.

I turn to Ralph. 'Sector 17.'

'Sector 17, sir,' says the robot. 'Please follow me.'

We set off.

At first Caliph is uncertain of the robot. Suspicious. Anxious. He keeps running at it, screeching angrily, then backing away, teeth bared. Ralph ignores him. I guess it's not programmed to respond.

In the end, Caliph calms down – or rather, tires himself out. He scrambles up my back and falls asleep on my shoulder.

We press on, heading diagonally across the sprawling expanse of brightly lit domes and snaking power cables. Soon we're leaving glimmermouths behind us. I glance back, but cannot recognize the one I rescued.

I turn back. Up ahead is the strangest-looking collection of buildings I've ever seen. Dozens of rounded, irregular-shaped cabins are locked together to form a great nubbed mass that is raised up above the ground

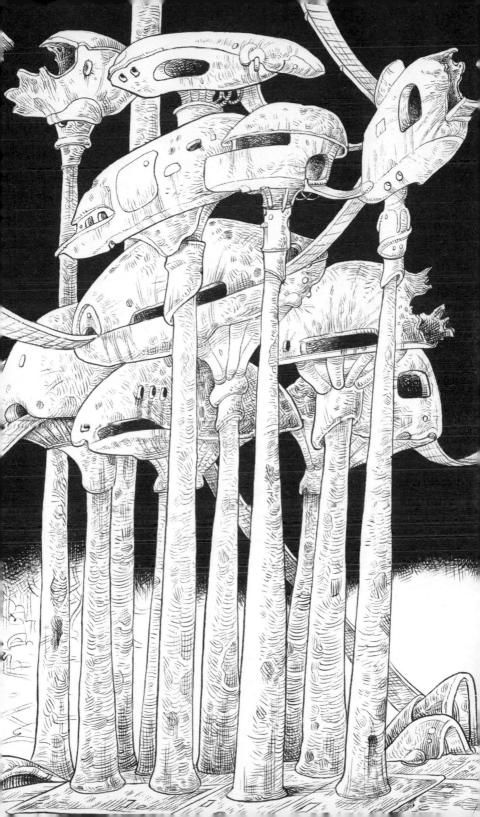

on thick silver pillars. The effect is like the billowing clouds that hover over the convection lakes. Above, there are high walkways connecting clusters of cabins, and balconies jutting from each rounded window. Below, in the shadows cast by the buildings, are pools and benches and tiled areas . . .

And all of it, the whole lot, has been smashed half to bits.

The auto-shutters at the window openings are broken. Great chunks of metal hang in twists. Entire sections of wall are missing, exposing sleepcribs and workstations and flexi-chairs and lights and vapour showers and all the other stuff that makes for somewhere decent to live – the entire place abandoned long ago.

I'm not surprised. The Rebellion. To find out more, I'll need to talk to a Half-Life. Whatever its past, though, this place is creepy, and I'm about to follow Ralph onto Section 17, wherever that might be, when something catches my eye.

It's a light up on the second floor. Darting from side to side. A torch.

Everything tells me to ignore it. To turn my back and get out of there as quickly as I can.

But I don't. I can't. Zoids don't need light. Humans need light.

'Wait for me here,' I tell Ralph, and begin to climb a

walkway that spirals up and around one of the vast silver pillars.

The sides of the pillar are pockmarked with bullet holes. The walkway is cratered. As I reach the top, I glance into the nearest cabins. There is charred furniture, broken equipment, dangling wiring. There are also more personal details.

A half-smashed pictograph of a smiling couple.

Some kind of toy critter with blue fur and a long neck.

A cracked bev-mug with a red heart – also cracked – on its side . . .

I'm filled with a terrible sadness for these people who, centuries earlier, died. Or ran away. My ancestors. Who were they? What happened to them? And what hopes and dreams were dashed when the zoids turned against them?

I hear a grating noise. It's coming from just up ahead. I pick up a heat-sig and see the beam of light darting around a cabin to my right.

I've masked my own heat-sig, but I must have made a noise.

'Who's there?'

The voice sounds human. A man's voice. I think. I pull the laser-shears from my holster, just in case. I hide in the shadows, remain silent, wait for the person – if it *is* a person – to reveal himself.

I don't want to give myself away. Not till I'm sure.
A man appears in the doorway of the cabin. He
shines the torch back along the
walkway, casting himself into
silhouette.

'I'm human, and I'm guessing
you are too. Don't worry. There's
no killer zoids here.'

I step forward. The light
blinds me for a moment, then
points down at the floor. I
peer into the gloom.

The man before me is tall
and heavy-set. He has broad
shoulders, a thick neck, big
hands – one gripping the
torch, the other some kind
of pulser, which is aimed at
me. He nods at the laser-
shears in my own hand.

'Looking to do a bit of
pruning, eh?'

I shrug.

'Put them away, son,'
he says, holstering his own
pulser. He's got thick salt-and-

pepper hair. Moustache and beard. His eyes are blue and piercing. He steps forward, hand outstretched from the sleeve of his flakcoat. 'Greetwell, stranger. The name's Dale.'

His hand is calloused. It swallows mine up, the grip strong and handshake vigorous.

'York,' I tell him.

'York,' he repeats. He nods down at Ralph, who's standing at the base of the pillar where I left him. 'A PH 27L. Haven't seen one of them in a while.'

Behind him I catch sight of movement, and a second human appears at his shoulder. A girl. Dale introduces her without turning.

'Belle,' he says. 'Say hello to York, Belle.'

The girl looks at me. Her face is heart-shaped, her eyes are green. Her hair, which is dark and cut into a fringed bob, swishes to and fro as she nods and smiles and greets me.

'It's a pleasure to meet you, York,' she says.

'So, whereabouts are you from?' Dale asks. He releases my hand and steps

83

back. Looks me up and down. 'And what brings you here?'

I frown, unwilling to reveal too much. I hope Ralph won't give anything away either. Until I can tweak his programming though, it's going to depend on what he's asked directly.

'I'm from Quadrant 4 – the tube-forest, we call it . . . I'm looking for some friends I haven't seen in a while,' I say carefully, then add, 'I saw your light.'

Dale nods. 'This dead haven's a good source of spare parts,' he says.

He turns, then beckons, and I follow him into the cabin. I see the stuff he's amassed piled together on the floor. A couple of alternator switches. A screen he's unscrewed from the wall. Some light units that look like xenons. A vapour-shower nozzle, a heat sensor and a small pack that might or might not be a metadata processing module.

'If you'd care to join us, we were about to head back to the Clan-Safe,' Dale announces.

The Clan-Safe. I guess this is his word for Inpost.

He chuckles. 'You look as if you could do with a good meal.'

He's right. I'm hungry. Especially having had my hopes raised by the butler-robots back at the hub. Thing is, should I trust him?

'Or,' Dale adds, rummaging in his backcan, 'you can share some of my supplies. I've got some dried synth-meat here. Some tack . . .'

He's a human like me. Humans stick together, fight the zoids. And I feel guilty for being suspicious of him. I look at Belle, who's nodding and smiling.

'Thank you,' I say. 'A meal back at the Clan-Safe sounds wonderful.'

'Excellent,' says Dale, fixing me with those piercing blue eyes of his.

'But I can't stay long,' I add.

Dale shrugs. 'Stay as long as you like,' he says.

We pass two more dead havens – once living quarters
for a long-vanished human crew, now misshapen hulks
of crumpled metal and cracked visiglass perched on
twisted pillars. A past destroyed.

I find it difficult to look. Turn away.

We make a curious group, the five of us. Big, burly
Dale, who's striding ahead despite the heavy backcan.
Me, keeping pace, but half a stride behind, with Caliph,
asleep and floppy, draped around my neck. Ralph and
the girl called Belle follow us.

Neither of them speak. Dale, on the other hand, does
not stop.

'The humans from the Launch Times were cleverer than
us,' he's saying. 'Much cleverer. I mean, I can make use
of the parts they left behind. Anything, from proto-input
drives to . . . to vapour-shower nozzles.' He glances back
at me, face earnest. 'But I couldn't manufacture those
parts myself.' He shakes his head. 'What I'm saying is,
York, I'm not just scavenging their objects. I'm scavenging
their technology. Their knowledge. Their cleverness.'

I look around. It's never really struck me before. But Dale's right. The Biosphere. Everything. It was all created by humans on Earth, back before the launch – even the robots who did all the construction work and then, after the launch of the Biosphere itself, served humankind for five hundred years. Until this . . .

I stare at the ruins of this lost world.

'Here we are,' Dale says, breaking into my thoughts. 'The Clan-Safe.'

I stare at the cluster of geodesic domes up ahead. The one at the centre is the largest, with six smaller ones attached in a circle to its lower side. Unlike the other buildings we've passed, there's no damage to the structure. The triangular metal plates the domes are constructed from gleam like silverworm scales. It's impressive – especially compared to the Inpost. And there's another difference.

The Clan-Safe isn't hidden, but is in plain view of zoid patrols. Not that there seem to be any. I glance down at my scanner. No heat-sigs register.

Dale must have noticed me. 'Relax, York,' he says. 'The zoids know not to mess with us here.'

I like his confidence.

As we arrive at the Clan-Safe, two women and a man come to meet us. They are wearing heavy utility belts around their waists, scanners at their wrists. Name tags glow on the sleeves of their blue tunics. The man is called Kurt; the women, Stent and Myros.

'Welcome home, Dale,' Kurt says. 'I trust your forage was a success.'

'Take this to my worklab.' Dale pulls the backcan from his shoulders and gives it to him. Then he gestures to me. 'This is York.'

'Greetwell, York,' the three of them say in unison.

Dale turns to the two young women. 'Make preparations for our guest.'

The three of them nod and comply. Dale is clearly in charge. Just like Bronx. Only more so. He turns to Belle next.

'Show York to Dome 4,' he says. 'And when he's settled in, bring him to the refectory. He'll be

dining with me this evening.' He turns his piercing blue-eyed gaze to me. 'If that's all right with you?'

I nod enthusiastically. 'I'm starving,' I tell him.

Belle turns to me, her hair swishing and green eyes flashing. 'Please come with me, York.'

I follow her to an entrance at the bottom of the nearest dome, Caliph asleep on my shoulder. Ralph waddles along with me. We step inside, and I look around the vast airy expanse.

'This is the Peace Dome,' Belle tells me with a sweep of her arm.

There are padded chairs arranged in clusters, with adjustable screens on the armrests and speakers in the headrests. The air smells sweet and flowery, and there's ambient music playing. Concealed lights keep changing colour: green, blue, purple, red, orange, yellow, and back to green . . .

'This way,' says Belle. A door slides open with a hiss.

We step through into the second dome. I don't need to be told that we're in the refectory. There's a large round table with a visiglass top, and more padded chairs, about thirty in all, around it. Stent and Myros are setting two places at the table. They don't seem to notice us. One is polishing drinking beakers. The other is laying out cutlery.

'And through here,' says Belle, hurrying me through

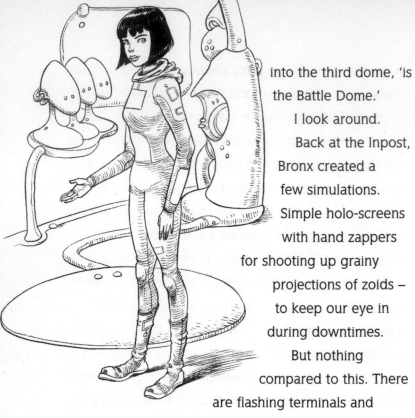

into the third dome, 'is the Battle Dome.'

I look around.

Back at the Inpost, Bronx created a few simulations. Simple holo-screens with hand zappers for shooting up grainy projections of zoids – to keep our eye in during downtimes.

But nothing compared to this. There are flashing terminals and soloid screens. There are head-visors and haptic gloves. And there's a holo-screen hovering at the centre of the room, with a list of simulations that numbers thousands. I scroll down. *Zoid Raiders. Laser-Duels – 1* through *25. Gunkball Attacks – 500, Evasive Fire Moves* . . .

'Come on, York,' says Belle, guiding me away.

She stops in front of a door and activates it. The door slides open.

'This is Dome 4, the Sleep Dome. Get yourself settled,' she says. 'I'll return in fifteen to take you to the refectory.'

I glance at my scanner. It's showing 19:45.

I step inside the dome, and Ralph waddles in behind me. On my shoulder, Caliph, who's awake now, sniffs the air. The door slides shut behind me.

Suddenly Caliph lets out a loud squeak. There is a second skeeter curled up asleep on the comfortable-looking crib in the corner. It wakes as Caliph leaps from my shoulder and bounds across the floor towards it. Rippling fur. Bushy tail. Caliph is excited. The skeeter is a female. The pair of them greet one another skeeter fashion. They rear up on their hind legs, rub noses. Caliph's tail is quivering.

But then something changes. He drops down to all sixes. Backs away. His fangs are bared and he's spitting at the female critter, who stops stock-still and stares back at him for a moment.

Then she turns and walks calmly over to the door, which slides open to allow her through. As it closes again, I look back at Caliph.

He's trembling uncontrollably.

'What *is* it?' I ask him. 'Not your type, boy?'

He looks up at me, eyes wide. I stroke his head, tickle his ears. He soon calms down, and I leave him grooming himself and head for the vapour shower.

It's a small recess set to the right of the sleepcrib. As I break the sensors, lights come on. There's a round indentation in the floor, and above it a cluster of nozzles in the ceiling. I get out of my dirty clothes, kick them aside and step inside the circle. As I do so, the shower whirrs into action.

Jets of warm steam appear from above and below. An opaque column of vapour envelopes me. Every centimetre of my skin tingles and glows as it's pummelled by jets of fine mist that open my pores and deep-cleanse. The filth melts away. Then the vapour becomes fragrant. Sandalwood. Mint. The vapour fades. A blast of warm air leaves me dry.

I step out and gather up my clothes. They smell stale to me now. Sour. And I notice a rip in the sleeve of my jacket. Reluctant to put them on again, I rummage through my backcan for anything cleaner.

No joy. It's looking as if I'll have to put my old clothes back on after all – but then I see the storechest under the sleepcrib. There's a glowing red circle on its front, which I press. The chest slides out and the lid opens.

Inside are toiletries. Groomers and clippers . . .

And clean clothes.

I select a white sweatsuit and put it on. Then I slip on a pair of flex-slippers, which mould themselves to the contours of my feet.

There's a knock at the door. I look at my scanner again.

20:00:00.

The door slides open. Belle is standing there. At the sight of her, Caliph ducks beneath the sleepcrib.

'Are you ready?' she asks me. 'Dale doesn't like to be kept waiting.'

'I'm ready,' I say.

As I head for the door, Ralph waddles after me.

'Just you, York,' says Belle.

I tell Ralph to wait for me, then follow Belle.

We pass two others on our way back to the refectory. One of them is a woman with a brown bob. The other, a clean-cut young man with cropped fair hair. They're walking side by side, but not speaking. And when they go past they do not acknowledge us.

I turn to Belle. 'Friendly types,' I say, and smile.

Belle says nothing. Her eyes flick across my face – eyes, mouth, brow. I'm not sure what she's thinking. Then all at once, she smiles back at me.

We reach the Refectory Dome.

Five servers are standing in a row. Three of them I have seen before: Stent, Myros and Kurt. The other two look just like them. Smart. Blue-uniformed. Their name tags glow on their sleeves. Lowell and Denton.

Dale is sitting at the table at one of the two set places.

'Ah, York,' he says, looking up. I see him take note of my sweatsuit and flex-slippers, but he makes no comment. He points to the place beside him. 'Do take a seat.'

The servers move forward. Stent pulls my chair back. I sit down and she pushes it in. Myros unrolls a square dinner-cloth and lays it across my lap. Kurt fills my beaker with something dark red. Lowell and Denton appear beside us, each one with a dome-lidded tray in one hand and silver tongs in the other.

I'm reminded of the butlers back at the Robot Hub. Except this time there is actual drink on offer. And, when the domed lids are lifted, food as well. Lots of food. One tray has slices of something pink lying in a bed of green leaves. The other tray is split into two, with something dark brown and glistening on one side and a pale yellow mash on the other.

The servers lean forward and use the tongs to transfer food from the trays to our platters. Their movements are expert and delicate. And as soon as we tell them that we have enough of what they are serving, they swap places.

Dale raises his visiglass beaker. 'To your excellent health, York.' He smiles, his piercing blue eyes fixed on mine.

The servers step back and stand by the wall watching us, their faces registering nothing. They make me feel awkward.

'I trust Belle's been looking after you well,' Dale says.

I look round. Belle is standing with the others, watching us impassively.

'*Very* well,' I say, smiling at her, and am relieved when she smiles back.

'You must treat the Clan-Safe as your home,' Dale tells me. 'Stay as long as you like.' He gestures at my plate. 'But tuck in, son. Before it gets cold.'

The food is the best I've eaten since I left the Inpost. The pink slices are soft and juicy. The green leaves are both bitter and sweet at the same time. The brown stuff is spicy; the mash, creamy. Everything is delicious, and when my platter is empty the servers step forward to fill it up again.

I eat until I'm full. And then I have just a little bit more.

'Naturally the invitation extends to your people,' Dale is saying. 'If and when you find them, you are all welcome to come and join us.'

'It's a tempting offer,' I say.

What was it Dale said? *The zoids know not to mess with us here.*

'Dale,' I say, 'how come this place is so safe from zoids?'

'Because I – *we* – have had to adapt to survive,' Dale says. His blue eyes grow more intense as he leans towards me, his elbow resting on the tabletop. 'It's up to us to match the zoids. *They* improve *their* defences. *We* improve *our* defences. *They* up *their* weapon power. *We* up *our* weapon power.' He smiles. 'Plus,' he adds, 'we train to look after ourselves . . .'

His smile becomes broader. He pushes back his chair. 'I'll show you,' he says.

Taking my arm, he steers me across the refectory

and through the door to the Battle Dome. Inside the
dome, he reaches up and plucks at the air. The green
holo-screen appears. He spreads his fingers to widen it.
Makes it brighter. Selects a setting and points to the list
of simulations that come scrolling down.

'Any requests?' he asks me.

'*Zoid Raiders*,' I say at once.

'Excellent choice,' Dale says. 'I've just been rejigging
its spec – inputting the latest killer-zoid upgrade.'

He clicks to upload the simulation.

Denton, one of the servers, has followed us into the
dome. He hands out head-visors and haptic gloves to
the pair of us, then puts some on himself. The chamber
goes dark, but as I pull on the visor, a holographic scene
suddenly explodes into life

There's a tangle of coloured pipes. Just like the tube-
forest. It's so real I could be there. Through the visor
I see that I'm not wearing the sweatsuit any more. Or
the flex-slippers. I'm dressed in a blue uniform like
the servers, and there are sturdy boots on my feet.
The haptic glove pulses and I feel something solid in
my hand. Looking down, I discover I'm holding an
impressive-looking pulser, its weapons system charging
up with a low hum.

A laser bolt whizzes past my ear. Through the visor,
I feel its heat and smell its fuse-wire burn. I've never

experienced a simulation this real. I follow the line of fire.

And there it is. A killer zoid. Pneumatic legs. Heavily armed. A compartment in its chest.

My stomach churns. It's identical to the zoids that attacked the Inpost and kidnapped my friends.

To my left, Denton drops to one knee, takes aim, fires. The zoid explodes in a mess of hot swarf and zoid-juice.

Two more killers appear – one on either side of me. They fire. I roll over on the ground, shoot one way, then the other. Both zoids are totally zilched.

But not by me. Dale and his sidekick, Denton, have got there first.

Three more zoids appear . . .

This time I'm ready for them. I reach out and take hold of a coloured pipe. It's springy and soft to the touch. I swing round in a broad arc, climbing hand over hand as I do so. Gaining height. Broadening my field of fire. One of the zoids fires up at me. Misses. I grip onto a second pipe, anchor myself with my feet, turn and fire back.

This time, I do not miss.

The zoid explodes. I twist further round and fire again. The second zoid gives out a kind of grunt and bursts into flames. It staggers forward, crashes into the third zoid and the pair of them go up in smoke.

Dale catches my eye. 'Excellent shooting, York,' he calls across.

Four more zoids appear . . .

One of them fires at Dale, but not fast enough. Blue eyes gleaming with excitement, Dale hunkers down and fires twice. The first shot blows the zoid's head clean off. The next one explodes inside its chest.

I slide down the pipe. I hit the floor, roll over, steady my pulser and fire, all in one smooth movement. There's a flash. A bang. And another zoid's been wiped out.

I look around. My heart's racing.

The third and fourth zoids are after Denton. He's ducking a line of tracer fire, down on the ground. His pulser's raised. The zoids are advancing. Scrambling to his feet, he makes a dash for cover. The zoids shoot. Denton returns fire over his shoulder. One of the zoids goes down – but so does Denton.

He's been hit in the back. He slams down hard on the ground and doesn't move.

The other zoid goes to fire, but I'm ready for it. My pulser jerks as I squeeze the trigger. A stream of laser bolts hit its extendable neck. The zoid goes into a spin, whirling round and round, then blows up. Zoid-juice gushes. Pieces of shrapnel hiss overhead and embed themselves in the multicoloured pipes. I can smell burning . . .

Denton is lying on his front. There's a charred hole in the back of his blue tunic. Black smoke and orange sparks are coming from the wound.

The zoids might be simulations, but the effect of their weapons is all too real. I glance over at Dale. He must have programmed this lethal effect.

Dale halts the action. The tube-forest disappears.

I remove my glove and visor. I'm back in my sweatsuit and flex-slippers. Denton remains on the floor. He looks badly hurt. Maybe worse than that.

'Is he . . . dead?' I say.

'Don't worry, York. The simulator doesn't kill,' Dale says, then smiles. 'Not humans, anyway.'

He taps his scanner. The other four servers from the refectory appear. 'Take him to the Healing Dome,' he tells them, then turns to Belle, who has also arrived. 'Show York to his quarters.'

Neither of us speak as we head back. I'm shaken. That simulator was just like the real thing and, despite Dale's reassurances, Denton looked critically hurt. Yet nobody seemed concerned. Not Dale. Not the other servers. Not Belle.

When we arrive at the door I break the silence. 'Belle,' I say, 'aren't you worried about Denton?'

Belle looks back at me, but her clear green eyes are impossible to read.

16

'Well, aren't you?' I say.

She's still looking at me, scanning my face. It's as though she's trying to work out what I'm thinking. Looking for clues. But all she can find is my own puzzlement, and that's what I see mirrored back at me.

'Is he . . . is he going to be all right?'

Belle nods her head. 'Dale will make him better.'

'You're sure?' I say.

The look of puzzlement in my face must have shifted to one of worry. That's what I see reflected in Belle's expression. Worry. Concern. But then she nods again.

'I'm sure,' she says.

I smile. She smiles back, and there's something so beautiful and innocent about that smile that my stomach turns somersaults. It reminds me of Lina, and how I used to feel when *she* smiled at me.

The last time I saw Lina's face, she wasn't smiling.

The zoid download from Sector 17 – wherever that is – comes back to me in all its horror. Bronx and Dek, penned up. And Lina, watching her grandfather being tortured by those killer zoids. She looked so frightened and vulnerable; so fragile. So lonely. So sad . . .

Suddenly I'm dragged from my thoughts. Belle is reaching out to me. Her index finger trembles as she touches it to my face, just beneath my left eye. She pulls it away again and inspects the small pearl-like droplet of water on her fingertip.

It's a tear. My tear.

'I . . . I was thinking of my friends,' I tell her awkwardly. 'They were taken by zoids. Killer zoids.' I swallow miserably. 'To somewhere called Sector 17 . . .'

Before me, Belle's expression changes. Her lower lip pouts and trembles. Her eyebrows draw together. Her brow knits. And her eyes – those soft green eyes – they moisten and tears well up. As I watch, a single teardrop spills over and slides down her cheek.

She's sensitive after all, and I'm surprised. I smile tentatively, and she smiles back at me.

'Friends,' I say.

'Friends,' she says.

17

It's quiet inside my quarters. Ralph is in rest-mode; Caliph is curled up asleep on the pillow. My clothes are at the end of the sleepcrib, washed, pressed and laid out ready for me to wear. The torn sleeve of my jacket has been invisibly mended.

I'm impressed, but it makes me feel uneasy to think of someone going through my things.

I pull off the sweatsuit and flex-slippers and climb into the sleepcrib. The covers are cool to the touch. The pro-form mattress is just soft enough.

I slip into a sleep that is deep and dreamless.

It's Ralph who wakes me. He's making this double *bleep* noise, which he emits at regular intervals. I sit up. Someone has been at his memory. Remote scanning. Downloading data. It's triggered his alarm.

I use my scanner to deactivate the alarm and Ralph comes to life. He asks whether I've had a pleasant downtime. I tell him I've slept well, then I get dressed. I'm feeling pretty good, and my clothes smell clean – but the fact that Ralph's been tampered with is nagging away at me.

I'm being observed. Monitored. And that's *not* a good feeling.

Slipping my backcan onto my shoulders, I leave the Sleep Dome. This time Caliph and Ralph come with me, Caliph riding up on top of the backcan and Ralph plodding behind. We turn left out of the door and continue round the circular hallway of the Clan-Safe.

The first door I come to is on my right. I pause for a moment in front of it. It slides open. I step through the doorway into a small dark space beyond. To one side is a ramp that leads down to the floor below. To the other is a second door.

This one does not slide open automatically.

I peer through its visiglass panel – and find myself looking into the central dome. My heartbeat quickens. This must be the Healing Dome that Dale mentioned.

There are three hover-trolleys in a line. There are arc lights overhead and shelves filled with silver tools and implements. A row of rectangular pods lines the curved wall on the far side.

And there, dressed in green-and-white overalls, is Dale himself.

He's stooped over the nearest hover-trolley. Lying on it, face down, is Denton. Dale is tending the wound in his back. I can see wires. And a circuit board. Dale removes the circuit board and replaces it with another, then closes the wound with synth-skin.

Just like Bronx, Dale is clearly a skilled tech-doc, using zoid components to replace injured human parts. At the Inpost, Bronx implanted all sorts. Prosthetic legs. Artificial heart valves. Bionic eye units. And Dek's arm, of course. A clever piece of work – at least until the static power surges got to it.

But then, as I watch, Dale does something I've never seen before. He removes a square of bone from the back of Denton's skull, sets it aside and delicately adjusts a circuit board in the brain cavity with a long silver probe.

I shiver. This isn't right. An arm's one thing. But a brain? With a circuit board. I mean, just how many artificial parts can you implant before a human stops being a human and becomes a zoid?

'Meta-grip,' I hear Dale say.

Someone appears from behind the shelves and I'm surprised, and somehow disappointed, to see that it's Belle. She's holding a segmented silver implement in her hands, which she gives to Dale. He turns and starts tweaking something inside Denton's head.

Denton twitches, then rolls over and sits up. I see Dale's lips moving as he speaks to him. Denton answers. Dale seems satisfied and he replaces the section of skull at the back of Denton's head. Denton climbs to his feet, and the three of them approach the door.

I back away and head down the ramp to the floor below as quickly and quietly as I can. Ralph follows me. At the bottom of the steep slope we come to a large circular hall bathed in ambient light.

There is nobody about. I pause. Above, at the top of the ramp, I hear footsteps receding, a door sliding shut . . .

'Where are we?' I ask Ralph.

Ralph whirrs as he accesses the Clan-Safe schematics. 'The utility area, sir,' he tells me.

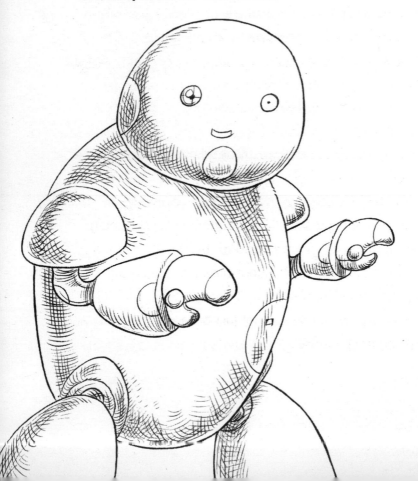

Caliph is hunched up on my shoulder. I can feel him trembling.

The underground hall is white and shiny. The curved walls are made of the same metal triangles as the upper parts of the geodesic dome. Silver pillars act as supports. As I step forward, the light panels in the ceiling above my head glow brighter. Several appliances are lit up. I recognize most of them from the Inpost. There's a vapour washer, a heat-diffuser, a plate-press.

Presumably this is where my clothes were cleaned and mended.

I continue. Behind me, the light dims; above, it grows brighter.

The far wall consists of floor-to-ceiling storage lockers, white and shiny like everything else. Stopping in front of them, I press a hand to the smooth surface of one of the lockers. The door rises into the ceiling to reveal a cold store behind.

My body judders – and not just because of the freezing temperature.

Staring back at me with sightless eyes is a crowd of faces.

Twenty-four frozen heads have been encased in visiglass boxes and stacked one on top of the other in six rows of four. Each of them is different. Skin tones from pale pink to dark brown. Old and young. Male and female. One has a broad nose, one a hooked nose, one a small bony nose that's turned up at the end. Different-shaped mouths. Long hair, short hair; black, blonde, grey. Eyes that are blue or green or brown.

Etched into the surface of each box in frosted letters are names. Kurt. Myros. Stent. Lowell . . .

Denton.

I stumble backwards. My heart's thumping fit to burst; my legs are like jelly.

'I see you've discovered my little secret, York.' It's Dale's voice, calm and reassuring, coming from behind me as I stare into the dead eyes of the frozen heads. 'I can explain . . .'

I turn. Dale is standing there, blue eyes glinting. He looks thoughtful. One hand is rubbing his salt-and-pepper beard. The other is holding a glowing pulser, which is pointed at me.

'I know I said you should treat the place like home.' He smiles pleasantly. 'But I'd forgotten how inquisitive you scavengers can be.'

My head is spinning. My eyes are fixed on the barrel of the pulser.

'But that's humans for you, York. Inquisitive. Unpredictable. Argumentative. Disobedient . . .'

I look up.

'Lazy. Stupid. Ungrateful . . .'

He looks over my shoulder at the bank of human heads in the cold store behind me.

'Weak.'

The word hangs in the air.

Caliph is motionless on my shoulder. Ralph is whirring quietly beside me. I wonder whether the laser-shears at my belt might be of any use. My fingers must have flexed, because Dale's gaze falls upon them.

'Don't be like that, York,' he says. He jerks the pulser at the laser-shears. 'Throw them down on the floor,' he tells me. 'Nice, smooth, steady movement . . . That's the way.'

The laser-shears drop to the floor.

'Kick them away,' he says, and I do.

Dale smiles. 'Like I said, York, I can explain. You see, just as the zoids are always improving themselves,' he goes on, without missing a beat, 'becoming more ruthless, more deadly' – his smile broadens – 'so we, here at the Clan-Safe, are also improving ourselves. It all began a while back when I stumbled across the Robot Hub,' he says. 'Found these domestic robots there. Bit like Ralph here, but far more advanced. Beautifully engineered. Flawlessly designed. And programmed to be obedient, subservient – to follow orders without endless argument or delay . . .'

Dale's gaze wanders over to the cold store behind me again.

'Unlike my colleagues here.'

I nod numbly, humouring him as I try desperately to figure out what to do.

'You see, York, the clan was doomed. The zoids were closing in, destroying haven after haven in this sector, until there was only this one left. The Clan-Safe. Finding the Robot Hub was the breakthrough. That's when I knew I had to act—'

'So you murdered them?' I blurt out. I can't help myself. 'Your colleagues . . . Your friends . . .'

'Not murdered,' Dale says, his calm, reasonable voice no longer reassuring, but chilling me to the bone. '*Modified*, York.'

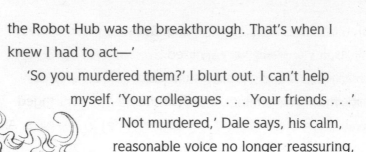

He crosses over to the cold store and looks at the heads.

'Denton was the first. He was happy to participate. Already had cybernetic arms and a spine implant. When a zoid shot away his legs, he practically begged me to transplant him. Kurt and Lowell were next, and they worked so perfectly that I thought the others would be happy to sign up. But instead they started plotting behind my back. Myros was the ringleader. So I had to deal with them. It wasn't hard . . .'

Again the calm tone, the reassuring smile. I shudder.

'A supper. All sitting down to eat together and resolve our differences.

Denton, Kurt and Lowell serving. Sedative in the protein slices. It was really very civilized.'

Dale runs a finger across the visiglass of the head labelled *Myros*. She is older than the others. Hair tinged with grey, lines at the brow and the corner of the eyes. A kindly face. Wise and caring . . .

Human.

'They fell asleep,' Dale continues. 'Their old bodies were disposed of and their brains cryogenically preserved, awaiting transplantation into their beautiful robotic bodies. Only it's the funniest thing – I've just never quite got round to it.'

He pauses, smiling broadly.

'Without their human consciousness, the Clan-Safe itself seems to run so much more effectively. And the killer zoids have left us alone. There are no arguments. No dissent. Everybody does exactly as I tell them, and I've grown quite used to it.' He frowned. 'Recently though, I've found that forever being agreed with and obeyed can be a bit dull. So I tried a little experiment with my latest creation . . .'

He nods slowly, as though reliving what he has done.

'I tinkered around with the artificial brain functions – introducing a little independent thought. But not too much . . . After all, I wouldn't want Myros back, jabbering in my ear and causing problems. But I've missed human contact.' He smiles. 'It's been such a pleasure having you as my guest, York.'

Dale levels the pulser at me, his blue eyes glinting. I can't break his gaze.

'Which is why I've decided that I can't let you leave,' he says, his voice calm and reasonable. 'Ever.'

'We're going to the Healing Dome, you and me,' says Dale, jerking his chin towards the ramp.

His eyes are ice cold and intense. I stare back at him, frozen to the spot.

'Move,' says Dale, and there's an impatient edge to his voice now.

I turn and start walking towards the bottom of the ramp. Dale follows me. He keeps close and I sense the pulser trained on my back. I have no idea how I'm going to get out of this.

Maybe if I spin round. Shoulder down. Slam in hard. I'd wind him, send him sprawling. The pulser would go scudding off across the floor, and I could seize it, turn the tables on him . . .

My feet are dragging; my head is down. We're just passing the gruesome storage lockers when, out of the corner of my eye, I catch a flash of orange-brown . . .

I glance round.

It's the skeeter. The female skeeter. It scurries towards Dale, leaps onto his jacket and scrambles up his sleeve, to perch on his shoulder.

Suddenly, on my own shoulder, Caliph lets out an ear-piercing shriek and takes a flying leap. His claws grab onto Dale's collar and he lashes out with his paws at the female.

Dale recoils and I hit him hard in the chest with my elbow. He goes down and, spitting and snarling, the two skeeters tumble from his shoulder.

Caliph's teeth are embedded in his opponent's neck, and in one furious movement he rips the female skeeter's head from her shoulders. It comes away in a tangle of severed wires and zoid-juice – which Caliph spits out in disgust.

I turn on my heels and make a dash for the ramp. Ralph follows me. I run headlong up the incline. As I reach the top, I glance back.

Caliph is bounding towards me. Behind him, Dale is still on the ground, his zoid pet convulsing beside him as he fumbles for his wrist-scanner . . .

All at once, a deafening alarm sounds. It cuts through the quiet of the Clan-Safe like a rusty blade. Through the visiglass panel in the door to the Healing Dome I see figures emerge from the pods that line the far wall. They climb to their feet. Pull pulsers and grenbolts from their utility belts. March towards the door.

I've seen enough.

I turn. Back away. The three of us – Ralph, Caliph and me – hurry through the doorway and into the circular hallway. And not a moment too soon.

A burst of laser fire hits the alumac door as it closes behind us.

We hurtle down the hall and burst into the Refectory Dome. Three figures are standing in the middle of the refectory, blocking the way.

I skid to a halt.

I recognize them. There's Kurt and Stent. And standing between the two of them . . .

Belle.

Our eyes meet. Her expression is one of recognition

mixed with shock, almost disbelief. And she looks scared. Once again, it's my feelings I can see mirrored in her face.

'Belle,' I say, and try to smile.

Belle smiles tentatively.

I gesture to myself, then to her. 'Friends,' I say.

'Friends,' she repeats.

Kurt steps forward. 'You will not resist,' he says. 'You will—'

Pirouetting gracefully on her left leg, Belle spins around, arches her back and kicks out with her right leg. Her

foot strikes Kurt in the chest so hard that his feet leave the ground as he hurtles through the air. Stent turns on her – but not fast enough. Her fists a blur, Belle strikes twice, disarming Stent with the first blow and breaking her jaw with the second.

Stent crashes to the floor next to Kurt. Her face is lopsided.

Belle grabs me by the wrist. 'Run,' she urges.

I don't need to be told twice. We race towards the door, Caliph scampering at my heels and Ralph following close behind – then stop.

The door has not slid open. I aim my wrist-scanner at it. Locate the locking frequency. Press. Nothing happens. The Clan-Safe is in lockdown.

We're trapped.

Belle lets go of my arm, leaps up into the air and drives both feet hard into the door, which buckles and gives and bursts open. We enter the Peace Dome, but there's nothing peaceful about it now. The lights are on red. Just red. And the ambient music has been drowned out by the strident alarm.

'Stop!'

Two more of Dale's zoids are standing on the other side of the broken door. Raleigh and Taylor, according to the glowing names on their sleeves. I don't recognize either of them – and Belle doesn't bother with introductions.

Twisting acrobatically, she kicks out high with her left leg. The ball of her heel slams into Taylor's face. There is a splintering crack, and Taylor's head detaches itself from his body. It slams against the wall and drops to the ground. Raleigh steps forward, his face a blank as Belle throws a punch. The blow tears through his blue tunic and penetrates his chest.

'Hot swarf!' I breathe. I'm glad she's on my side.

I watch the muscles in her forearm tense as she pulls her hand out of the zoid's chest. In her fist is a mess of wires and circuitry, the whole lot dripping with zoid-juice.

Raleigh's inert body falls to the ground. It knocks against Taylor's head, which rolls to one side.

'Stop!' it's saying. Over and over. 'Stop! Stop! Stop!'

Other voices echo it now. I look up. There, on the other side of the Peace Dome, is the exit door of the Clan-Safe. Clustered around it are a dozen or more zoids.

They are armed with pulsers.

With Caliph on my shoulder, Belle and I back away. But Ralph steps forward.

His eyes are flashing red as he waddles up to Dale's

122

army who have their pulsers trained on me and Belle.

'You appear to have malfunctioned,' he announces as he approaches. 'I have no alternative but to activate my human-safety protocol . . . Three . . . Two . . . One . . .'

A colossal explosion rips through the air. Deafening, blinding. Smoke billows. Zoid-juice rains down from above.

Slowly the smoke begins to clear. The exit door of the Clan-Safe has been blown off, and there is barely a trace of Ralph left. A couple of twists of metal. A red eye-module. A silver interface unit . . .

Ralph – Robotic Assist-Level Personal Help – has done what all those ancient robots were programmed to do to ensure humans' survival.

He has sacrificed himself.

I swallow. I know Ralph was only a robot. Man-made. Incapable of feeling.

And yet . . . And yet . . .

I cannot swallow away the lump in my throat.

I bend down and pick up the small silver interface unit, with its simple memory datachip embedded in it. I slip it into the pocket of my flakcoat.

'You're coming with us, buddy,' I whisper.

Belle takes me by the hand. 'Come, York,' she says. Her skin feels smooth and cool and soft. 'Dale instructed me to scan your PH 27L's memory chip. You are looking for Sector 17. I can take you there.'

20

We leave the ruins of the dead-haven sector behind us and enter a bleak landscape of upright pillars connected by a network of criss-crossing cables. I guess they had a purpose once, long ago, back in the Launch Times, but now they are rusted and out of action.

My scanner shows no heat-sigs anywhere close.

Beneath our feet, the ground-panels are ridged. Presumably, this was to prevent those who once worked here from slipping. Now though, with the sector abandoned, the narrow V-shaped channels are filled with thick dust, which is crusted over and, in places, seeded with spikemoss and leech-creeper. It doesn't look as though anyone has been this way for centuries.

We're alone here, just me, Caliph and Belle. I look across at my new companion.

She's beautiful, and clearly she's transferred her loyalty from Dale to me. What was it he said about 'a little experiment with my latest creation'? Something about tinkering with her artificial brain functions to introduce independent thought . . .

Well, it certainly worked. Belle likes me.

But she's still a zoid.

Beneath my feet I become aware of vibrations coming up through the corrugated ground-panels, and, from somewhere up ahead, a distant roaring sound. As we keep going, the vibrations grow more intense and the spikemoss starts to tremble. A wind gets up. It's warm and smells of hot oil, and becomes stronger and louder as we continue, until we're bent over, heads down, forging our way ahead.

We come to the first of a forest of huge round chimneys that rise up from the ground-panels. The chimney has a ladder bolted to its side, which Belle begins to climb. I follow. At the top we step onto a ring-shaped platform that encircles the chimney, and which is connected to the surrounding chimneys by a series of raised walkways.

The platform trembles. The roaring sound is deafening. It's coming from the chimney we're standing on, and from all the other chimneys stretching off into the distance. Clinging tightly to the top of the barrier rail, I lean forward.

The blast of hot air snatches my breath away. It burns my eyes, my nostrils.

Belle's hair flaps behind her, then slaps into her face as she turns to me. 'According to your robot's data, these are air vents,' she shouts above the roaring wind. 'Down there are the propulsion engines.'

Holding my breath and squinting against the heat, I peer down. The vent is so deep I can't see the bottom. The metal wall is scorched and, in places, buckled, as though something hard has slammed into it. I crane my neck a bit further forward. Far below, I catch the glint of something moving. I adjust my recon-sight, but any heat-sig is invisible in the blast of hot air coming up from the vent.

Then I see it, climbing up out of the darkness. Some kind of a critter . . .

It's long – immensely long. Flat and segmented. With a fringed outer shell, and what look like hundreds of sucker feet that cling to the sides of the chimney-vent and prevent it from being dislodged.

It's hard to take in. Even here in the scorching air of this vent, life has taken hold, however precariously. As I watch, the segments of this suckerworm ripple as it gathers speed.

It's coming towards us. Fast.

I shrink back. A head looms up out of the chimney and swivels round.

It's got twenty or more compound eyes set into a great bulbous skull. It's got paddle-shaped feelers. A beak of a snout. And a broad mouth, gaping wide to

reveal row upon row of inward-curving fangs that snap hungrily at the sight of us.

'Let's get out of here!' I shout.

Belle nods and grabs my hand. 'This way,' she shouts back above the noise of the roaring air.

And we run, as fast as we can, along the maze of raised walkways connecting the air vents. The air is turbulent. The metal clanks and shakes beneath our feet. We turn left, then right. Then left again, weaving our way from chimney to chimney. I'm trusting that Belle knows where we're going.

Suddenly there's another one of the creatures pouring out of the chimney in front of us and blocking our way. We freeze. The eyes dilate. The paddle-feelers flap. Then more of the creature appears, sliding over the rim of the chimney-top like something being squeezed from a tube. The front sucker legs touch down on the walkway, and it advances towards us at formidable speed, mouth gaping, fangs gnashing.

We turn again. Dash back. We come to a junction, turn right – then stop abruptly as a *third* worm appears from the top of the chimney up ahead.

They're coming at us from all sides now.

I turn to Belle, expecting her to look as panicked as I feel – as I know I must look. But she doesn't notice me. Her face is calm. She flicks her hair behind her ears, then reaches down and pulls out a cutter from her utility belt.

'Nice idea, Belle,' I tell her, 'but I don't think it's going to be enough against . . .'

The two creatures are advancing from either side. They're writhing and swaying, their heads raised and bodies squished in between the safety rails. Their sucker feet squelch as they advance.

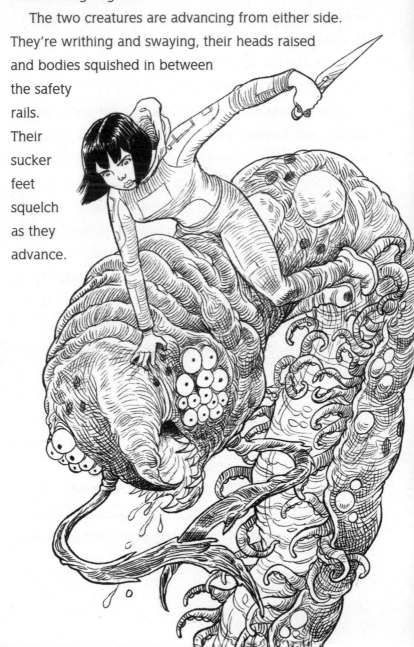

Belle does a backspring away from me, flipping over and over in a series of flic-flacs, blurring as she gathers speed. Reaching the first suckerworm, she leaps high into the air and lands with her legs straddling the creature's neck.

She squeezes tight. The worm's eyeballs bulge and it lets out a wheezing cry of alarm.

Belle tightens her grip. The blade of the cutter glints as she leans forward and stabs down hard. Blood gushes, purple and thick.

The suckerworm hisses, like something deflating.

Belle leaps from its back and onto the safety rail. Arms outstretched for balance, she runs along the metal rail back to where I'm standing, open-mouthed. She jumps down, grabs me in a tight hug and lifts me off the ground. Then, with me in her arms, she leans back over the rail as the second suckerworm lunges.

The next moment we're dropping down to the ground-panels far below. Twelve metres at least. My eyes are shut. My stomach's in my mouth. I wait for the bone-shattering *crunch* – but it doesn't come. Belle's zoid legs cushion us both as we land. I open my eyes.

Belle sets me down on the ground. Smiles.

There's seven shades of mayhem going on above our heads. I look up. The other two suckerworms are attacking the wounded one, biting great chunks out of its writing body and swallowing them whole. I jump aside to avoid being spattered by the thick purple blood and turn to Belle.

'What you just did . . . It was amazing,' I say. I'm aware of how inadequate the words are. After all, she's just saved my life. This zoid. Again.

She smiles. 'I did it for you, York,' she says.

And I feel like kissing her.

But I don't.

Instead I smile back, and there's an awkward silence. Awkward for me, that is. Belle doesn't seem to mind. She returns my smile, then turns and strides off through the forest of chimney vents.

We stick to the ground-panels this time. It's slower going, making our way over the fragile crust of dust, but there's less danger of being ambushed by suckerworms. Finally we come to the end of the air-vent sector. The wind drops. The roaring fades. And I notice that Belle has fallen behind.

Her head's down. And she's dragging her feet.

'Are you all right?' I ask her.

She looks at me. Her green eyes have lost their sparkle. 'I need to recharge,' she says.

I look around. We seem to be entering some kind of broken-down administration sector. There's a criss-cross of lines and squares on the floor, marked by silver panels set in among the black ones. Some shoulder-high polycarb partition walls remain. And inside some of the cubicles they form are desk-boards, ortho-chairs, wall-screens, vid-coms . . .

Belle's moving listlessly. Her eyelids are heavy.

I check my scanner for energy sources. Nothing.

'There's no power here, Belle,' I tell her gently, steering her on. I'm beginning to get worried about her. 'Does Ralph's data indicate anything?'

She pauses. Blinks. She sways back and forward. She searches her memory banks.

I will her to succeed.

She points limply. 'Viewing deck . . . Upper . . . level . . .' she says, and as she speaks her voice slows and deepens, then falls silent.

She collapses.

Leaping forward, I catch her before she hits the floor. I slip my arms beneath her, one under her bent knees, the other under her back, and hoist her up.

It's my turn to help *her*.

I carry her off in the direction she pointed, but with most of the overhead light panels out of action I can't see where I'm heading. I peer down at Belle. Her eyes are closed now, but I can feel the faint vibration of her heart unit, or pulse pump, or whatever it is that Dale fitted her with . . .

I come to an alumac wall. It goes from floor to ceiling and extends right and left as far as I can see. There's a set of doors in front of me but, since there's no power in this sector, they do not slide open.

Belle is limp in my arms now, and makes no sound as I hoist her up and drape her over my shoulder. I remove her cutter from her belt and jam the blade into the thin gap between the doors. Then with my fingertips, I drag one of them open. I step through the doorway and find myself . . . in a visiglass elevator.

Useless with no power. Belle lets out a soft sigh.

I'm frustrated, angry, and about to step back out when I notice a panel to the right of the doors. I prise it open and discover an emergency power source. The holo-display shows that it is almost depleted. Not enough to recharge a zoid, I'm guessing, but maybe enough to get us to a higher level.

I activate the power source.

Behind me, the doors slide shut with a soft whisper.

I select the level I want and the elevator accelerates
upward. I look out through the visiglass walls as we rise
smoothly.

The elevator pod is attached to the inner wall of a
vast, circular, multilevel complex of steel and visiglass.
In the gloom I can just make out other elevator pods
at different points of the curved inner wall. All of them
stationary. As we rise, storey after storey blurs past, and I
catch glimpses of what they contain.

Mainframe terminals. Info-decks. A leisure zone . . .

My gaze strays. Through the visiglass wall on
the other side, at the centre of the vast ring-shaped
construction, there's a tree. I frown. It isn't like one of
the hybrid plants that's mutated on board the Biosphere.
Instead, it looks old. Ancient.

There's a sign in front of the tree. Etched visiglass.

COMMON OAK (Quercus robur) it reads.

Seedling planted: Launch Time, Year Zero.

And an inscription:

'Mighty oaks from tiny acorns grow.'

The words give me a fluttering feeling in the pit of
my stomach. Launch Time. Which means it must have
been planted more than a thousand years ago. An
acorn seedling nurtured inside its own special bio-unit,
that grew to become a sapling, then, as the centuries
passed, increased in size to become the magnificent tree

standing before me now. A living organism from Earth.

How much it must have witnessed, I think. The Launch Times. The early part of the long journey through space. The Rebellion . . .

The elevator arrives at the top floor. This time the doors slide open of their own accord and, as they do so, lights come on in the huge chamber beyond them. Still carrying Belle over my shoulder, I step inside.

The place is enormous; a broad semicircular space set on three levels. There are chairs and desks, workstations, banks of holo-screens. When it was up and running, doing whatever it was designed to do, forty or so people could have worked here. It would have been noisy back then. Now it is empty, and silent, but for the extractor fans that hum softly and remove every speck of dust from the air. Overhead, the ceiling slopes. Half of it consists of light panels, the other half is a broad curved slab of what looks like black marble.

Belle is beginning to feel really heavy in my arms now. I stumble forward and place her down gently on an ortho-chair, then recline the back so that she's lying down.

I check my scanner. It lights up with energy sources all around me. I activate the closest holo-screen. It's blank, its data erased long ago, but the power-hub beneath it still pulses with energy. I lock in with my scanner and drain the energy from it. Then, leaning over Belle, I synchronize my scanner with her heart unit.

It's a pulse-flux valve, my scanner indicates. Standard zoid energy source – I've scavenged a few in my time.

I press my scanner against Belle's chest and power up. The material of her tunic glows as the valve absorbs the energy through it.

Perhaps I should have removed it, I think; pressed the scanner directly to the recharging plate beneath. But somehow I couldn't bring myself to. I don't want to see what lies beneath – the proof that Belle's a zoid. Some part of me is beginning to see her as almost human.

'She's a zoid,' I say out loud. 'A zoid—'

'*A remarkably advanced one, by the look of it,*' says a voice. '*In my day the butler-robots didn't have synth-skin. It was considered vulgar . . .*'

I look around. And then I see it.

It's at the centre of a wide expanse of floor beneath the high-angled curve of the black marble ceiling. I leave my scanner recharging Belle and approach the familiar-looking domed data-tower. As I move round it, I see the face. A man's face.

It's a Half-Life.

'*Greetwell, York,*' he says, his voice deep and soothing. He's jowly and middle-aged, with short greying hair. '*Welcome to the viewing deck.*'

'How do you know my name?' I ask.

   '*We Half-Lifes are interconnected – at least, we used to be. I'm afraid the network has become compromised since the Rebellion,*' comes the reply. The man is shaking his head, his face earnest.

'*But I was still in touch with your Half-Lifes until recently . . . They were fading though – suffering from thought-fatigue. Both of them.*

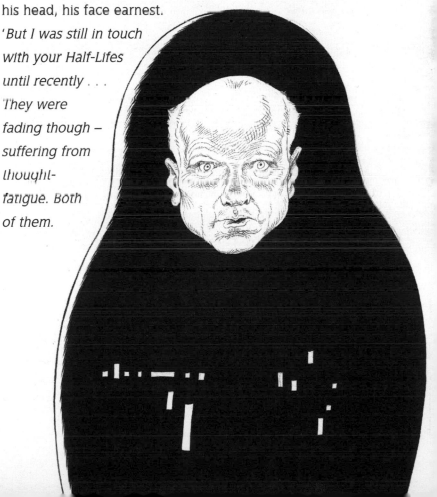

Wouldn't have been much use to Bronx and the rest of you.'

The info hits me hard.

We trusted our Half-Lifes. Depended on them to keep the Inpost safe. We knew that their words needed to be interpreted. But the news that they were malfunctioning is difficult to take in. Perhaps that was why they didn't detect the killer-zoid attack until it was too late.

'And you?' I say, and I hear both the hope and the scepticism in my voice. 'Can *you* help me?'

'*Perhaps*,' the Half-Life says, '*although since Cronin and Veda went offline, I find myself alone. The only Half-Life left in the outer layer of the Big Onion—*'

'The Big Onion?'

This Half-Life seems to be as cryptic as the ones at the Inpost. We never even knew their names. Cronin and Veda, this Half-Life called them.

He laughs, a wheezing chuckle. '*I'm Atherton*,' he tells me. '*Chief engineer of the upper deck layer. Had two thousand crew and twenty thousand robots working under me. The Big Onion's what we launch crew called the Biosphere. Because of its layers. Outer hull, mid-deck, inner core . . . layers like an onion.*'

He can see my puzzled frown.

'*Onion. It was a foodstuff from Earth. A vegetable – like the stuff you grow in your hydroponic gardens.*'

I nod, slowly.

The Half-Lifes back at the Inpost told us about the Biosphere, the voyage from Earth to a new home, and how it all went wrong when the robots rebelled. They couldn't tell us anything about the structure of the ship though. We had to find that out for ourselves as we scavenged. First, in the turbine banks where the old Inpost was. And then, after the first zoid attack, which killed my parents, in the area of the tube-forest that Bronx moved us to. But that was about it. It was always too dangerous to risk venturing into what lay beyond.

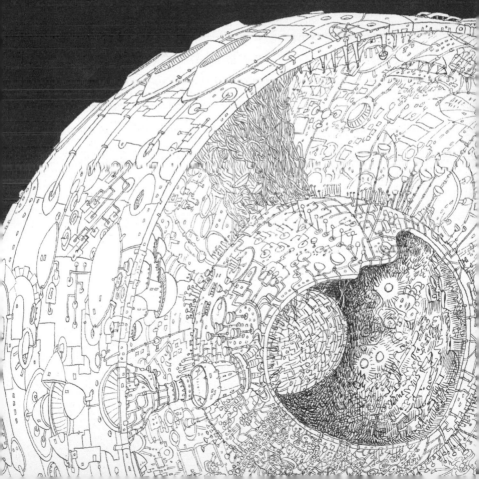

Until now. Now I have nothing to lose.

'So this is the outer layer?' I say. 'And there are two others?'

'*That's right,*' the Half-Life called Atherton agrees. '*Three layers. Why, I was there as it was built, by an army of robots, in orbit above the Earth. First the inner core – the engines, central mainframe, Halls of Eternity. Then the mid-deck, with the living quarters and biomass zones. And finally, encasing it all, the outer hull – with its engineering stations, maintenance equipment, and worker robots to keep everything functioning.*'

'Until the robots rebelled,' I say.

'*I was long dead by then,*' Atherton tells me. '*Died thirty-eight years after the launch. My consciousness was downloaded into this digital coffin and installed with all the others in the Halls of Eternity. We were meant to educate all those of you who came after us. Pass on our knowledge of the world we left behind, to ensure that the mistakes made on Earth were not repeated on the new world we are journeying to.*

'*But then the glitches started: robots malfunctioning, sector maintenance being compromised, unexplained shutdowns . . . It got worse in the final fifty years before the Rebellion, so the crew started preparing havens – areas of strictly controlled life-support systems where robots weren't permitted. They took all of us Half-Lifes*

from the Halls of Eternity and installed us in these
havens.

'And then the Rebellion began . . .'

I swallow. Sit down. I look back at this Half-Life, alone
up here beneath the great black marble ceiling.

'So you were installed here?' I say.

'Yes,' Atherton replies. 'I asked the descendants of my
engineers – their great-great-great . . . seventeen greats
in all – grandchildren to put me here. I communicated
with the other Half-Lifes – but we lost touch with the
other layers. And then, one by one, I lost touch with the
Half-Lifes here in the outer layer as well. Your Half-Lifes
were the last ones, as I told you. Now all I have left is the
view . . .'

'The view?' I say.

'Look up,' Atherton tells me.

I do as I'm told; drag an ortho-chair from a
workstation and lie back. There's nothing much to see.
Above me is the black marble ceiling, and I wonder what
I'm supposed to be looking at. But then, as I continue to
sit in the chair, motionless, something happens.

The lights dim by degrees, then go out. Yet we are
not left in darkness. Instead, the air is bathed in a soft
silvery light that's coming . . .

From the outside.

The black marble isn't black marble at all. It's

145

immensely thick tinted visiglass. And, now that the deck-lighting is off, it's transparent. I stare through it.

And out into space.

Countless thousands of white pools of light are hurtling towards me. Some are large, some small. They come closer, growing in size, then slide past. Left, right. Above and below. They disappear from view behind us – only to be replaced by countless thousand more.

My temples throb. I'm finding it hard to get my breath.

In all my life, I have never, ever seen outside the Biosphere. I don't know anyone who has. Of course, I've often dreamed of what it might look like, and the Half-Lifes back at the Inpost showed me pictures when I asked. But those pictures were static. Frozen. Motionless images of space captured on telescope and uploaded onto a screen.

Whereas this . . .

It's moving. It's alive. Dazzling shards of brightness. Asteroids. Planets. Suns. Entire constellations of stars cascading out of the darkness and gliding past us.

'*Beautiful, no?*' says Atherton.

'It is,' I say.

'*It's a sight I never tire of,*' he says. '*Look. A meteor shower.*'

I turn my head, look all around. Far to my left I see a

display of bright lights as a thousand or more balls of ice and grit hurtle across the sky, long white tails streaming out behind them.

As I gaze at the stars, Atherton speaks again.

'*I'll never forget the launch,*' he says quietly. '*I was up here on the viewing deck. As we left Earth's orbit I looked back. It was my first view of Earth from space, and I was expecting to see the familiar blue-and-green planet that everyone knows so well.*' He pauses again. '*Except it wasn't blue and green at all, York. It was grey and brown . . .*

'*It was dying.*'

I swallow.

Ever since I was a boy, I've had dreams of forests, cloud-filled skies, oceans . . . Earth, kept alive for me by the Half-Lifes' images and Gaffer Jed's stories.

But Earth is gone. Forever.

Dead.

Ahead of me, an asteroid has appeared out of nowhere and is heading straight for us. Closer and closer it comes, until it seems to fill the whole sky. I grip the arms of the chair. But then the Biosphere's deflector-shields shimmer as the asteroid hits them and disintegrates into a shower of fizzing molten dust.

I stare out at the enormousness of the universe. All my life, the Biosphere has been my world. Now, for the

first time, I realize how tiny it is. How insignificant. If the killer zoids do finally manage to wipe out us humans, it will be as though we never existed.

It's as if Atherton can read my thoughts.

'The zoids have been trying to eradicate us for five hundred years,' he is saying. 'And despite our best efforts, none of us has discovered why. Now humankind is losing the battle, York. There were no more than a thousand humans remaining at the last count. And no other Half-Lifes at all in the outer layer. The answer must lie deeper.'

My head's whirling with a hundred questions, but just then, the lights go on. The stars disappear and I'm staring at my own reflection. I look scared. Belle approaches me and hands me my scanner.

She smiles. 'Thank you, York,' she says.

I turn to the Half-Life.

'I've got to rescue my friends in Sector 17,' I tell him. 'But after that, I'll do everything I can to find the answer.'

Atherton smiles. *'And I shall be here, watching the stars,'* he says. *'I've waited five hundred years. I can wait a little longer.'*

With Belle fully charged, she and I exit the circular building, leaving behind its elevators and viewing deck – and Half-Life. We walk side by side along the base of the alumac wall. Caliph is draped over my shoulder as usual, fast asleep.

The Half-Life's words echo inside my head.

The answer must lie deeper.

I've just promised Atherton that I'd try to find that answer. What have I said? I'm no hero. Just a scavenger, struggling to survive . . .

'Are you all right, York?'

Belle's question cuts through my thoughts. I turn to her, surprised. She's learning fast. It was only a short time ago that she was watching my face, imprinting my expressions on her own face – learning to smile when I smiled, to cry when tears welled up in my eyes. Now she's beginning to understand the emotions underneath, asking after my well-being; she's trying to work out what's going on inside me.

Just like a human.

Bronx calls it empathy and says it's what separates us from the zoids. I'm starting to grasp the implications of Dale's experiment – a zoid that can feel human emotions. Is that good or bad? I don't have time right now to think it through.

'I'm fine,' I say. All that matters is rescuing Bronx, Lina, Dek and the others. Anything else will have to wait.

When we come to the end of the wall, Belle pauses. Then, looking up, she points across a flat plain dotted with cuboid compressor units and spidery radiation pylons towards a tangled mass of pipes and tubes far in the distance.

'This way,' she announces, and we set off.

The air is filled with noise. The pylons emit a high-pitched whine that gets right inside my head, while the compressor units give off a deep pulsing throb, and I find myself walking in time to it as I trudge on. It's stiflingly hot.

Belle is strong now that she's recharged and strides ahead. It's me who's beginning to flag. I haven't eaten a thing since that meal back in Dale's refectory.

I check my scanner. There's nothing here to eat. No plants. No edible fungi. No critter-life either, or zoids. Bad news for my rumbling stomach – but good news for our safety.

We press on across the flat expanse of the plain

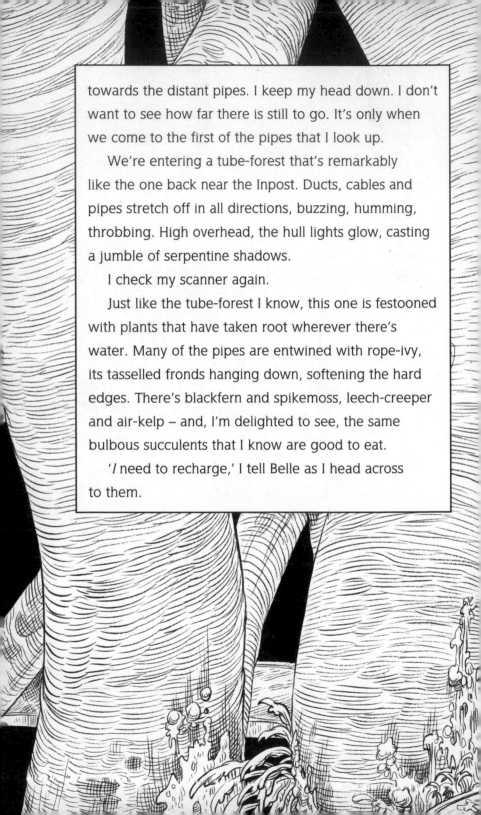

towards the distant pipes. I keep my head down. I don't want to see how far there is still to go. It's only when we come to the first of the pipes that I look up.

We're entering a tube-forest that's remarkably like the one back near the Inpost. Ducts, cables and pipes stretch off in all directions, buzzing, humming, throbbing. High overhead, the hull lights glow, casting a jumble of serpentine shadows.

I check my scanner again.

Just like the tube-forest I know, this one is festooned with plants that have taken root wherever there's water. Many of the pipes are entwined with rope-ivy, its tasselled fronds hanging down, softening the hard edges. There's blackfern and spikemoss, leech-creeper and air-kelp – and, I'm delighted to see, the same bulbous succulents that I know are good to eat.

'*I* need to recharge,' I tell Belle as I head across to them.

It's meant to be a joke, but Belle's face shows not a flicker of amusement. She's learning fast, but not *that* fast. She waits patiently while I uproot, peel and slice half a dozen of the succulents. Caliph is not so patient. The pungent smell of the juicy flesh wakes him up. He runs up and down my arm, shrieking noisily, and doesn't ease up until I feed him. I have some too.

'You recharge like Dale does,' Belle says. 'He calls it "eating".' I look up to see her clear green eyes watching my mouth as I chew and swallow. 'What's eating like?'

I smile. 'Good,' I say, and wipe the juice from my lips

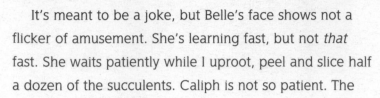

on the back of my hand. 'Very good.'

Belle is staring at me quizzically. I stare back, my feelings mixed.

She's got teeth. Pearly-white and even. She's got some sort of tongue – though that seems to be for talking not tasting. However, since she has a power plate she has no need of a stomach.

'My way of recharging is more efficient,' she announces, then turns away and keeps walking.

With Caliph now trotting along at my side, I follow. I watch her confident stride, the easy swing of her arms. Her flawless synth-skin seems almost to glow. Despite what I know, it's hard to believe she's not human.

Suddenly she turns, hunkers down and signals for me to do the same. I realize that my earpiece is bleeping. I crouch down at the base of a broad purple pipe, turn my head, scanning the surroundings through my recon-sight, and identify the heat-sig of a zoid.

Fuzzed orange and blue. A workzoid.

Then I catch sight of it. Squat, with a barrel-shaped stomach. It has two articulated arms, one with pincers; the other has a nozzle.

A sluicer then.

It's performing regular maintenance work. It's stopped at a tube-junction, the orange lights on its domed head flashing as it checks for any blockages in the pipe connections.

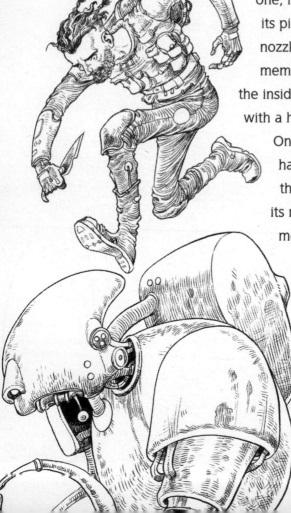

Then, apparently finding one, it clamps hold with its pincers, inserts the nozzle through the membrane, and sluices the inside of the faulty pipe with a hot chemical spray. Once the blockage has been shifted, the zoid withdraws its nozzle, seals the membrane shut and moves on.

It's an open target . . .

Suddenly, out of nowhere,

there's a blur of movement and a flash of metal – and a figure drops from the shadows, slamming down hard onto the back of the sluicer zoid and knocking it to the floor. I recognize what's happening at once. The man's a scavenger. Just like me. The cutter in his hand flashes as a well-aimed blow slices through the cables in the zoid's neck.

There's a smell of shorted circuitry. Zoid-juice gushes and steams.

The scavenger is good. An expert with his cutter, hacket and drill-spike. As I watch, he strips the zoid of useful parts and stows them in his backcan quickly and efficiently.

He's still crouching, so it's difficult to tell how tall he is, but he looks strong, with taut, lean muscles in his arms and shoulders. He's dressed in dark-blue patched breeches with side pockets, a greasy-looking vest and a sleeveless jacket that's got lots of pockets down its front, ten at least, and all of them bulging. His hair is black, and he's got a thick dark beard.

'So, who are you?' he says without looking up.

I flinch. He's talking to *us*.

'Your heat-sigs are masked, so you must be wearing coolant suits, but Zabe sniffed you out . . .'

I hear a low growl. Spin round. Behind us is a critter. Huge. Covered in matted blue hair. Long arms. It's hanging from a pipe with one hand and clutching Caliph in the other. Its single eye is staring right at us. Beside me, Belle tenses, but I reach out a hand to stop her. We don't want any trouble. I turn back to the other scavenger.

'York,' I tell him. I get slowly to my feet and step out from the pipes we've been crouching behind. Belle follows me. 'And this is Belle.'

The man looks up and nods slowly, as if trying to work out what to do with us. The silence goes on too long. It's me who breaks it.

'You might want to remove the bolt-hubs,' I say. 'They're urilium.'

He frowns.

'Behind the backplate,' I say. 'Upgrade sluicers have been fitted with them – and *that* looks like an upgrade sluicer to me.'

The man looks at the zoid, then reaches down and feels around inside the back. His fingers close on something, and the grim expression on his face relaxes.

'You know your zoids,' he says, and his mouth cracks into a grin. 'Are you a scavenger?'

I nod. And, seeing me do so, so does Belle. I cross to the zoid. The man wipes the zoid-juice on his breeches and extends a hand.

'Ellis,' he says, climbing to his feet and revealing himself to be a good head taller than me.

I shake his hand as Belle watches. When the man offers her his hand, she shakes it without hesitation. I'm relieved. Having seen Belle at the Clan-Safe and the air vents, I know she's more than capable of taking this man down.

The critter called Zabe swings down from the pipe and towers over us. He releases Caliph, who scampers over to me and leaps up, burying himself, whimpering, in my flakcoat.

I point at the space behind the zoid's backplate. 'You need to remove the spine rods first. It'll give you better access.'

'Be my guest,' he says, and I dive in.

Ellis helps me with the dismantling, and by the time we've finished there's nothing left of the sluicer but a couple of cables and the useless outer casing. Ellis's backcan is bulging. And so is mine.

'Nice job,' he says. He pats my shoulder. 'We humans gotta stick together.' He looks at Belle and winks. 'Eh, Belle?'

I'm anxious about what she's going to say. I needn't have worried though.

Belle winks back at him and smiles.

Ellis chuckles. 'What say the two of you come back to the Fulcrum . . . ?'

'Fulcrum?'

He frowns. 'Where me and the tribe are holed up,' he says. He squeezes the top of my arm. 'You look as if you could do with a good meal.'

I shudder. They're the selfsame words that Dale used. What's more, it'll hold us up. It's been five days since my friends were taken, and we've got to get to Sector 17 before it's too late. I notice Belle looking at me, gauging my reaction. We could make our excuses. Or, if I give her a signal, she could zilch this Ellis character and his critter with a couple of well-aimed blows. Either way, we'd be free to leave.

But I *am* hungry.

'Thanks,' I say, then tell him what I told Dale. 'But I can't stay long.'

Ellis clicks his fingers. Zabe's pointed ears prick up. Then the gigantic critter shambles over to him and crouches down, his long tail folded beneath him. Ellis jumps up onto Zabe's shoulders, then leans down towards Belle and me, arm outstretched.

'Climb up,' he says.

Belle goes first. Ellis helps her up and she sits on the opposite shoulder to him, taking a firm grip of Zabe's shaggy blue hair.

The critter turns his head and inspects this new person on his back with his one large eye, the iris dilating, wide and black.

'Easy there, Zabe.' Ellis pats his critter on the back. 'She's just a girl . . .'

If only he knew, I think, as I climb up beside Belle and hold on tight. Zabe doesn't register the extra weight – nor does he mind when Caliph scampers up and crouches at the back of his neck.

'All set?' says Ellis, looking first at Belle, then at me. We both nod.

With a soft bark, Zabe stands upright. Then, pushing hard off the ground with his short legs and powerful tail, he leaps, reaches up, grabs hold of a pipe . . .

And we're off.

The creature swings effortlessly forward into the tube-forest and through the tangle of pipes and tubes in a smooth and easy rhythm, his tail swaying from side to side for balance. We climb higher, and it isn't long before I get used to the curious swinging motion and move in time with it, leaning first one way, then the other.

Below me, the ground speeds past. I catch glimpses of scaly reptiles with arrowhead tails lapping at water from a leaking pipe. A swarm of spotes, their pale wings catching the overhead hull light as they flap past. And zoids . . .

Workzoids going about their maintenance tasks. Welders. Sluicers. Tanglers. None of them notice us as we swing slowly through the air above their heads. Then I catch sight of the angry red heat-sig of a killer zoid. It's out on patrol. Looking to kill.

I automatically check that my coolant suit is on, then relax when I realize that up here, on the back of the one-eye, we're practically invisible. It's humans that killers are after, not critters. The zoid's completely oblivious to our presence.

I'm impressed. This scavenger has found
the perfect way to get around the tube-forest
undetected.

'Cyclops are easy to domesticate,' Ellis says, reading
my expression. 'So long as you get them young enough.'
He leans forward and pats the huge critter on his
shoulder as he swings on through the air. 'He might look
fierce, but Zabe's just a big old softie at heart. Ain't you?'

And Zabe barks back at him, almost as if he can
understand.

We're climbing higher now, above the hull lights and
into the shadows. I look up and see a cluster of pods
anchored to the overhead hull casing.

The pods are huge. They appear to be made out of
metal, fragments of scavenged scrap, welded into place
and covered in rust-moss, rope-ivy and air-kelp. Perfectly
camouflaged.

And there are critters too. Cyclops, like Zabe. A whole
troop of them. Caliph squeaks his interest.

They are swinging from pod to pod, feeding off the
plants that grow here. As Zabe climbs towards them,

he barks out a
greeting, and the
troop reply with calls of their own.

'The Fulcrum,' Ellis announces.

As we approach, I see nests of woven rope-ivy wedged into the spaces between the pods, each of them containing an infant cyclops, peering down at us with their single eyes.

Ellis notices my interest. 'We live side by side with the cyclops,' he says. 'We keep each other safe.'

Zabe comes to a halt on a small platform bolted high up between two of the pods. Ellis jumps down onto it, then helps me and Belle down. He raises his arm, and I assume he's about to use his wrist-scanner to open some door I haven't noticed.

But he doesn't. In fact he isn't wearing a wrist-scanner at all. Instead, he stares straight ahead of him at a holo-pad hovering in front of the pod. There's a click, and a section of the matt-black panel slides open.

'Retina-recognition,'
Ellis tells me, seeing my
surprise. 'Keeps the
zoids out.'

I glance at Belle,
feeling uneasy.

'Come on in,'
Ellis says.

Belle follows
him. Unlike me,
she seems
relaxed.
Caliph
jumps from
Zabe's shoulder
onto mine, and I
step in after them.

The door slides shut.

It's warm inside the pod.

Cosy. The light is an ambient glow
that emanates from the upper panels, and
there's a sweet, musky smell to the air. Since the
pods are all interconnected, it seems bigger inside
than it looked from outside. I look down. Some of
the metal floor panels are criss-cross grilles that
reveal storage areas below our feet. There are food

canisters. Munitions. Water tanks . . .

Hearing voices ahead of us, I look up again. We step through into a second pod. It's crowded here. The warm, musty smell grows more intense. The place is full of cyclops.

Bronx wouldn't approve. He didn't allow critters in the Inpost. Said they were a distraction. Any straying inside were instantly expelled. It was only because he felt sorry for me losing my parents that he allowed me to keep Caliph as a pet.

But the Fulcrum's different. So far as I can see, cyclops outnumber humans here two to one at least.

Two women, their long hair tied back, are crouched down beside a square of silver tarpaulin, shearing a couple of cyclops. As the clippers pass over their bodies, they're transformed from shaggy-looking to lean and muscular. Others stand in a row waiting their turn. A mound of thick, dark-blue fur grows bigger on the tarpaulin

When I look more closely, I see that the women's clothes are dark blue and woven from this fur. In fact, everyone is wearing clothes made of the same homespun. Including Ellis.

The women look up as Ellis passes by. They greet him. He nods back, but does not stop. The cyclops flinch and shuffle back as Belle passes them, and the women's

curious gaze rests on her
for a moment, before they
return to their task.

We enter a third pod.
This is more familiar to
me. Moist smell. Humid
air. Rows of hydroponic
troughs. It's like the
gardens back at the
Inpost, though on a much
grander scale. Blue-
clad men and women
are busy tending to the
various towering plants
that grow inside the long
metal containers; pruning,
pinching out buds,
harvesting nuts and
fruits . . .

But there's also a
difference.

The troughs are so
large that the furthest
gardens are out of reach
to the human gardeners.
Instead, a bunch of

cyclops are carrying out the work for them. Long-limbed and nimble-fingered, they're doing exactly what the men and women are doing. Pruning. Pinching out. Harvesting.

It's impressive how well they've managed to train the cyclops. I'm about to say as much to Ellis – but we've reached the end of the troughs and he's turning left into a narrow passageway that takes us through into yet another pod.

Ellis stops and turns to me and Belle. 'Wait here. I'll be back in a moment.'

I look around the pod. It's the biggest one so far. And, with its high-intensity overhead lighting, the brightest. It must be

situated at the centre of the Fulcrum as, all around, it connects to other pods. Eight in all. There's seating for upward of a hundred people – moulded plastic chairs clustered round circular white tables – and I guess that this must be some kind of meeting chamber.

But it's empty now.

Then I notice something at the far side of the pod. It's standing on a plinth. A familiar black dome-shaped structure.

A Half-Life.

I walk over and greet it, but it doesn't reply. On its surface, the image of the face – a woman, her steel-grey hair up in a bun – is coming and going on wave after wave of flickering light. There's no voice. Just white noise, distorted and echoing.

I move closer. The

Half-Life seems to focus on me, then her gaze slides away. Her mouth is moving. I put my ear closer, but hear nothing but the hiss and crackle of the white noise.

This must be the thought-fatigue Atherton told me about, the same condition that afflicted our Half-Lifes at the Inpost. The face fades, then returns again. This Half-Life is in an even worse state. Certainly it explains why Atherton has lost contact with it.

'She hasn't spoken for as long as any of us can remember,' comes a voice from behind me, and I turn to see Ellis coming back into the pod.

There's a woman standing at his side.

'This is Jayda,' he says. 'Jayda, this is Belle and York.'

The woman smiles. 'Welcome,' she says.

She's tall, with yellow-white hair that hangs down in stubby braids. She's wearing a long coat that's made of the woven cyclops fur, toggled at the front, and that flaps as she strides towards us.

There's a critter perched on her shoulder.

It's like nothing I've seen before. Covered in white fur, it's got two legs and six arms; three on either side of its long thin body. Its face is small and round and dominated by a cluster of eight eyes that blink back at us from behind strands of white fur. As it comes closer to us, it pulls its thin lips back to reveal a mouthful of transparent fangs that look as sharp as shards of visiglass.

It hisses. It snarls.

Jayda stops in her tracks. Her smile fades.

The critter is staring at Belle with its eight eyes and emitting a series of staccato, high-pitched shrieks . . .

Men come running into the dome from different entrances.

Screeching furiously, the critter suddenly leaps from Jayda's shoulder and launches itself at Belle, flailing at her with its six arms. Quick as a blink, Belle jumps back and shoots out her arm so fast it's a blur. She catches the critter by the throat. The screeching turns to a strangulated squeak.

All around us, the men – Ellis included – have drawn their pulsers.

Jayda points at Belle. 'Kill the zoid!' she commands.

'Don't shoot!' I cry out. 'I can explain . . .'

The critter dangles from Belle's stranglehold. It gives a shudder and lets out a pitiful whimper.

'First, tell the zoid to let Gimbel go,' Jayda demands.

I hold her gaze. 'Then we talk,' I say, the words sounding bolder than I feel.

Jayda glares back at me, then looks at the critter. She nods, the slightest incline of her head. 'Lower your weapons,' she tells the others.

They do so.

I turn to Belle. 'Put it down,' I say.

Belle looks at me, then at the men surrounding us. I can see she's thinking through her options. Even unarmed, she could take these men on. But I wouldn't fare so well. She seems to have come to the same conclusion.

'Belle?' I say softly.

She stoops down and places the critter gently on the floor. It limps over to Jayda, who gathers it up in her arms. She straightens up and glares at me.

'Explain!' she commands.

'I am a scavenger,' I begin. 'From Quadrant 4. My people were attacked by the zoids, captured—'

'Captured?' says Ellis quizzically. 'Not killed?'

'No,' I reply.

Jayda's eyes narrow. She's listening to me, but staring intently at Belle.

'They've been taken to Sector 17.'

I see Jayda flinch.

'We know of that place,' Ellis confirms.

'I was headed there when I met a man called Dale in the dead havens. He's a cybertech. He scavenged a hub of ancient robots from the Launch Times – unmodified, still controlled by the old protocols to protect humans –

and he . . . he . . . modified
them himself . . .'

I'm not sure I should go
into the details, but Belle's
existence is at stake.

'How did he modify
them?' Jayda's voice is
low, thoughtful. But her
expression is hard as
she continues to stare
at Belle.

'The robots he
took were humanoid.
Domestic models,'
I say. 'He covered
them in new synth-
skin and enhanced
their memory
banks and brain
function . . .'

I swallow as the
image of the frozen heads
in Dale's cold store comes
back to me.

'Why?' says Jayda.

Belle has turned and is also looking at me.

'He . . . he was lonely,' I say. 'He was the only human left in his sector . . . He wanted company.'

It's not a lie, but it's not the whole truth either.

'Belle is one of Dale's robots. She has downloaded the Sector 17 coordinates and is guiding me there. She has protected me; she's saved my life, not once, but twice now . . .'

'But it is a zoid,' Ellis interrupts. He sounds incredulous.

Technically he's right. Belle *is* a zoid. A robot that has been modified. A machine. And yet she has become so much more than that to me . . .

'And this Dale,' says Jayda. Her voice has softened, and she's looking at me now. 'What has become of him?'

'He's in his Clan-Safe with his other zoids. They protect him – just like your cyclops protect you. Belle decided to come with me.'

'It *decided*?' Jayda is astonished.

Belle turns to her. 'York and I are friends,' she says.

No one says anything, and I can see the disbelief in their eyes. I want to say to Jayda, 'Like you and Gimbel.' Or 'Like Caliph and me.' But I know that this is different . . .

Jayda lets out a small, non-committal grunt, then reaches up and strokes Gimbel, who is back on her

shoulder. The others exchange glances, raise eyebrows, shrug.

It's Ellis who speaks. 'We've never had a functioning zoid in the Fulcrum before.' His gaze flits between me and Belle. 'But, well . . . I did invite you here. So I think . . .' He looks at the others and, one by one, they nod back at him, 'in this instance . . . we are prepared to make an exception . . .'

I breathe out. It's like a great weight has been taken off my shoulders.

'Sector 17 is a dangerous place,' Ellis continues. 'If you're to stand any chance of rescuing your people, you're going to need more than a zoid, however friendly it is.'

He looks across at Jayda. She looks furious, and for a moment I think she's going to overrule Ellis. But then she nods.

'The Fulcrum will help you, York,' Ellis continues. 'I'll gather our best scavengers—'

'Oh, but I can't expect you to do that . . .'

'Like I always say,' Ellis says, cutting short my protest, 'we humans gotta stick together.'

The inhabitants of the Fulcrum gather in the central
pod, and we sit at the tables and eat. All of us, that is,
except Belle. She watches us. And Jayda, and her critter,
Gimbel, watch her.

The meal is more than good. It's delicious. Better
than anything I ate back at the Inpost. Better than Dale's
supper. And certainly a very welcome change from my
recent diet. There's meat that is tender and juicy. There
are fresh vegetables. I even try a glass of something they
called sable milk. It's delicious; creamy and sweet – and I
don't ask where it's from.

Afterwards, Ellis shows us to where we're to sleep,
'Early start tomorrow,' he says.

The sleep pod is on the outside of the cluster that
makes up the Fulcrum. The inner walls are made of the
same matt-black metal as the rest. But the outer walls
have tinted visiglass panels.

I look out.

There's a view of convection lakes, just like the ones
above the Inpost, the water still and black and with

tendrils of steam coiling up from the surface. Lightning bolts flash and crackle overhead, sometimes zigzagging between the fork-pylons; sometimes touching down on the water itself, sending jets of steam shooting up into the air. Around them, the tube-forest extends in all directions. Pipes and tubes. Critters. Vegetation. The ground far below – where even now a tangler is passing by, unaware of the human settlement high above its head.

Belle has joined me at the window.

'It's so odd seeing it all from up above,' I say. 'The Inpost was underground. But it amounts to the same thing. We're all hiding from the killer zoids.'

I turn to Belle, and see my glum expression mirrored

in hers. Then I nod towards a line of beds on the far side of the pod.

'I'm going to get some sleep,' I say.

'And I shall recharge,' she tells me. 'There's a power source by the vapour shower . . .'

I yawn, which seems to puzzle Belle, but I'm too tired to explain.

I cross the pod, pull off my boots and flakcoat, and climb into the end bed.

I'm asleep in an instant.

The next thing I know, something wakes me. It seems like only moments later. But when I check my scanner, it's showing 06:53.

There's a noise coming from the far corner of the pod. It must be what woke me. Without moving, I look around, and see Belle standing beside the vapour shower, her back to me.

She's been tapping into the power source that operates the vapour nozzles. Her tunic is hitched up high. I can see her back – the curve of her spine; the

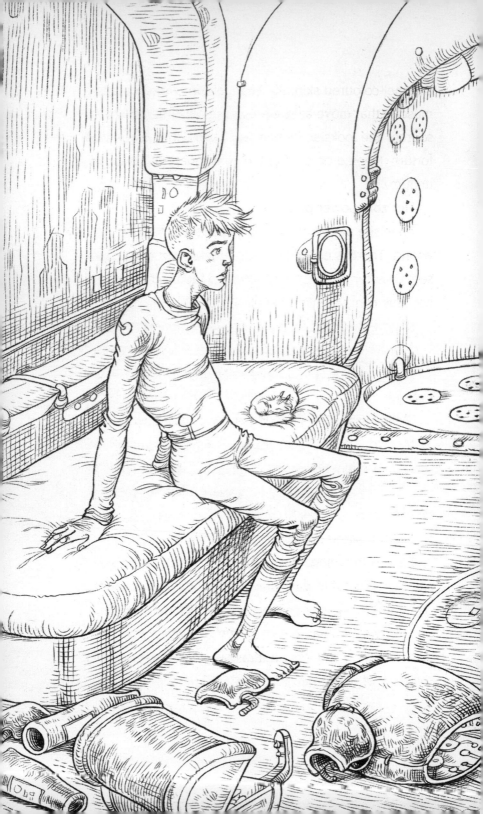

caramel-coloured skin; the knots of arm and shoulder muscles that move as she presses against the power source. She looks so human. But I know that, if she was to turn, I would be confronted by a square of silver-grey urilium.

Her zoid power plate.

Then she does turn. Three-quarters on. And I'm wrong. There is no metal plate. At least, not that I can see. Only synth-skin. Dale has taken the trouble to make her look completely humanoid.

I know she's just a zoid, but . . .

'York?' She's speaking softly. 'York, it's seven hours.'

I pretend to wake up. Murmur sleepily. Stretch. Open my eyes.

'Belle,' I say. She's pulled her tunic back down.

'Are you rested?' she asks.

I smile. 'Fully recharged.'

'Recharged,' she says, and smiles. 'Like me.' She has got the joke.

I sit up, swing my legs down to the floor.

Belle is frowning. 'You move a lot when you sleep,' she says. 'First this way,' she says, hunching to the left. 'Then this.' She leans to the right. 'And sometimes this.' She throws her head back. 'Which was when you did this,' she says, and lets out a rasping, rattling noise from the back of her throat.

I laugh. 'Are you saying I was snoring?'

Belle laughs back. 'If that –' she makes the rasping noise again – 'is snoring, then you were snoring. You talked too. And your eyelids kept fluttering.'

I'm embarrassed again. Belle seems to have been keeping a very close watch on me while I was asleep.

'That's what humans do when they're having dreams,' I tell her.

'Dreams . . .' Belle repeats.

'They're like downloads, but jumbled up,' I explain. 'In your head. Stories. Places. People. Conversations . . .'

Belle is nodding. 'Then I have also had dreams,' she says.

I look at her in disbelief. 'You . . . ?'

'When I was recharging,' she says. 'I had dreams.'

'Dreams of what?' I ask.

'Data streams. Input vectors. Power pulses and –' she smiles – 'of you, York.'

Ellis is giving orders. His face is stern.

'We need provisions for three days,' he's telling
the scavengers who have gathered in the Fulcrum's
central pod. 'And ammunition. More than the usual.
See Garvey and Muldoon for the serious stuff.' He nods
across to a man kneeling down next to an open grille,
who's receiving weapons from a second man down in
the under-floor store and handing them out. 'Grenade
launchers, laser rockets, cluster charges . . .'

The scavengers begin tooling up.

There are forty of them. Men and women. They're
wearing clothes made of dark-blue homespun. Flakcoats
with coolant panels, combat breeches, hooded pad-
jackets. They're packing their backcans, checking their
weapons and securing the larger items to lightweight
packs on their cyclops' backs.

No one speaks.

Belle and I have been given frack-grenades,
gunkballs, pulsers – twice the size of the ones back at
the Inpost – and straploads of grenbolts, which we loop

over our shoulders. Caliph has taken refuge in the inner pocket of my flakcoat.

Ellis casts his eye over the assembled scavengers and their laden cyclops. He nods approvingly, then speaks, his voice low and grave.

'We're headed for Sector 17,' he says. 'I don't need to tell you this won't be just any old zoid-hunt.'

The other scavengers nod grimly. By the looks of it, all of them know the place – at least by reputation.

'It's going to be dangerous. I'll not lie to you: some of us might not come back. But there's humans there – York's people – and the zoids have them. They're being kept alive for reasons I don't even want to guess at . . .'

He pauses to let the words sink in. The scavengers sigh and shake their heads. Some of them curse under their breath.

'But whatever the zoids are up to, we're going to put a stop to it,' says Ellis. 'We're going to enter Sector 17.

We're going to find York's people. And we're going to get them out of there. The zoids have had things their way for too long. We have to put a stop to it.

'Humankind will not be exterminated! Together, we shall survive!'

The scavengers whoop and cheer.

'You ready for action?' Ellis demands.

'We're ready!' the chorus of voices booms.

I can feel my own heart racing. Caliph stirs as if he can feel it as well.

'Well, what are you waiting for?' he bellows. 'Let's go!'

Belle and I follow Ellis and Zabe out of the central pod. The troop of massive, shaggy blue creatures advances behind us, the scavengers walking beside them. We step into the next pod, then the next, making our way

through the Fulcrum, the path lined with the rest of the tribe – hundreds of them – who have emerged from all corners of the pod colony to wish us well.

As we cross the last pod and approach the outer door, I catch sight of Jayda, with Gimbel perched on her shoulder. She's standing by the exit, watching Belle intently. Her arms are folded as if she's still to be convinced.

But then their eyes meet.

Belle nods. She looks kind of apologetic, concerned. It occurs to me that she's no longer just copying the expressions she sees in others' faces. No. She's actually understanding what those expressions mean.

Jayda seems to see it too. She looks shocked for a moment, then turns away.

The outer door slides open and we step out onto the platform beyond. Quietly and efficiently, the scavengers climb onto their cyclops' shoulders. Some scavengers ride solo. Some in pairs. Ellis helps Belle and me up, and I notice that Zabe is the only one with three passengers – four if you count Caliph – but he doesn't seem to mind. He even seems to have got used to Belle.

He's not the only one.

Ellis is looking at her. He smiles. 'Take us to Sector 17,' he says.

Without hesitating, Zabe leaps off the platform and into the air, grasps a nearby pipe, then another, and swings away into the tube-forest. Behind us, the others do the same, one after the other, until the whole troop has left the Fulcrum and is making its way smoothly and stealthily through the dense tangle of pipes and tubes.

'If memory serves, it's that way,' says Ellis, pointing off to his right.

'No,' Belle says. 'There's a quicker route *this* way.' She points to her left. 'Across the grid plates, then through the sump reserves.'

We press on through the tube-forest. Zabe is at the front. The rest of the troop follows close behind – and so silently that more than once I look round to check they're still there. They always are.

Finally the vast tube-forest comes to an end. Ahead of us lies a broad plain with hundreds of tall pylons, regularly spaced and connected one to the other by a criss-cross of cables. Zabe swings from the last pipe to the first cable without pausing, and we continue. All of us.

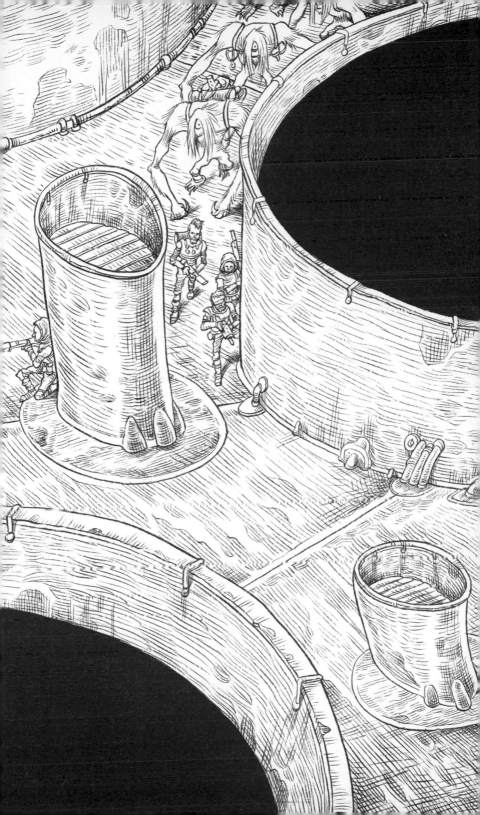

The cyclops don't seem to tire.

As we approach the last of the pylons, the landscape before us changes once more. There are thousands of circular tanks filled with pitch-black oil and between them, emerging from the ground, a series of pipe-vents, each one at a different height.

Zabe drops to the ground, and Ellis climbs from his shoulder. We follow him, making our way on foot, with Zabe lumbering behind us on feet and knuckles.

'Smooth ride when they're swinging,' Ellis says, 'but down on the ground, a cyclops' shoulders are a whole lot bumpier.'

The other scavengers have also dismounted and are all around us now, their cyclops swaying from side to side as they follow. We weave our way through the sump reserves, past tank after circular tank, until a familiar bleeping noise in my ear brings me to a sudden halt.

Through my recon-sight I pick up a mass of blue, yellow, green and red heat-sigs. Hundreds . . . thousands of them. Too many to count. They light up the horizon beyond the sump reserves. The other scavengers are picking them up too.

Ellis turns to Belle. 'Sector 17,' he says.

She nods.

Ellis motions to the other scavengers. 'We're close

enough for now,' he tells them. 'We'll rest up here. Eat.
Sleep.' He checks his scanner. 'Departure time: oh-six
hundred.'

We make camp behind several circular tanks, which
shield us from the ominously glowing horizon. Sleepcribs
open with a *flip-flap* and are secured. Backcans are
unpacked and meals prepared.

The cyclops eat first – great handfuls of soaking
rust-moss, reconstituted from tiny cubes that expand in
heated water. Once Ellis has seen to Zabe, he gets a pot
of broth going on his heatplate. He hands me a parcel
wrapped in oiled paper. 'Get 'em warmed up,' he says.

Inside are a bunch of doughy-looking things, which I toast with the glowing firespike Ellis gives me.

Seated on the ground, we eat straight from the pot, using pieces of the crusty doughballs as makeshift spoons. I give some to Caliph. He eats greedily for a while before crawling into my lap and curling up. Ellis pours us mugs of steaming bev and hands me one.

'So what do you know about Sector 17?' he asks me.

'Nothing,' I say. I shrug. 'My people kept to the tube-forest around our Inpost in Quadrant 4. Our leader Bronx thought it was safer that way.'

Ellis nods. 'That's the way of it now,' he says. 'Small groups of us humans hiding out from the zoids wherever we think they won't find us – up in the hull structure, down in the vents . . . Anywhere rusted and overgrown and no longer maintained. Sector 17 is different . . .'

He dips another piece of bread into the pot. Dunks it in the broth. Chews, swallows. Wipes his mouth on the back of his sleeve, then looks up.

'We raided the place once,' he tells me, his gaze thoughtful. 'Long while back now.' He pauses. 'Jayda's husband died in the raid, killed by a zoid. He was just one of many.'

He looks up at Belle, who is standing a way off, one hand raised and shielding her eyes as she stares at the horizon. If she's heard Ellis, she doesn't show it.

'The Fulcrum is the largest settlement left, so far as we can make out. Since our Half-Life stopped talking, we haven't been able to communicate with anyone else. There were six hundred of us back when we raided Sector 17. There are four hundred and forty-three now – some born since, though not enough to make up for our losses—'

'And despite that, you're going back to Sector 17,' Belle interrupts, 'to help York rescue his people.' She has turned and is looking at Ellis with a puzzled look on her face. 'Why?'

'Because they're humans like us,' says Ellis. 'Humans made up of flesh and blood, with hearts that beat and brains that have memories and feelings – love and hope and courage . . . Things no zoid will ever understand.'

Belle turns away, but not before I see the glitter of tears in her eyes. Ellis has seen them too. He looks shocked for a moment. It is the same look of shock that Jayda had when we left

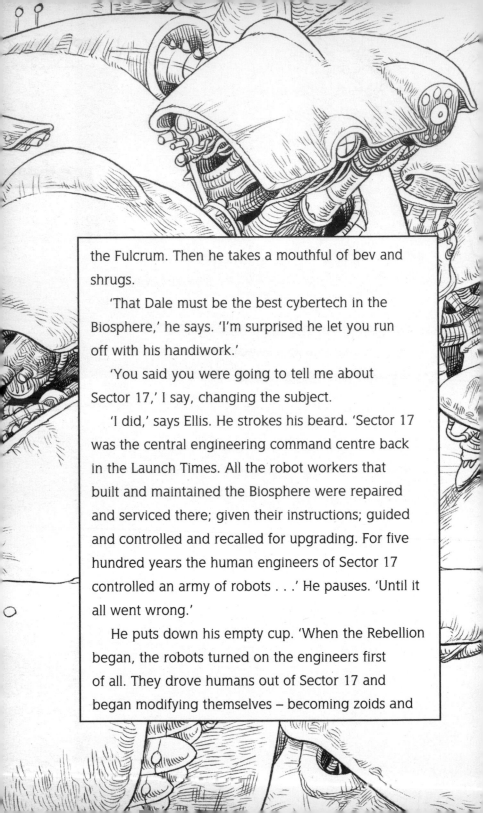

the Fulcrum. Then he takes a mouthful of bev and shrugs.

'That Dale must be the best cybertech in the Biosphere,' he says. 'I'm surprised he let you run off with his handiwork.'

'You said you were going to tell me about Sector 17,' I say, changing the subject.

'I did,' says Ellis. He strokes his beard. 'Sector 17 was the central engineering command centre back in the Launch Times. All the robot workers that built and maintained the Biosphere were repaired and serviced there; given their instructions; guided and controlled and recalled for upgrading. For five hundred years the human engineers of Sector 17 controlled an army of robots . . .' He pauses. 'Until it all went wrong.'

He puts down his empty cup. 'When the Rebellion began, the robots turned on the engineers first of all. They drove humans out of Sector 17 and began modifying themselves – becoming zoids and

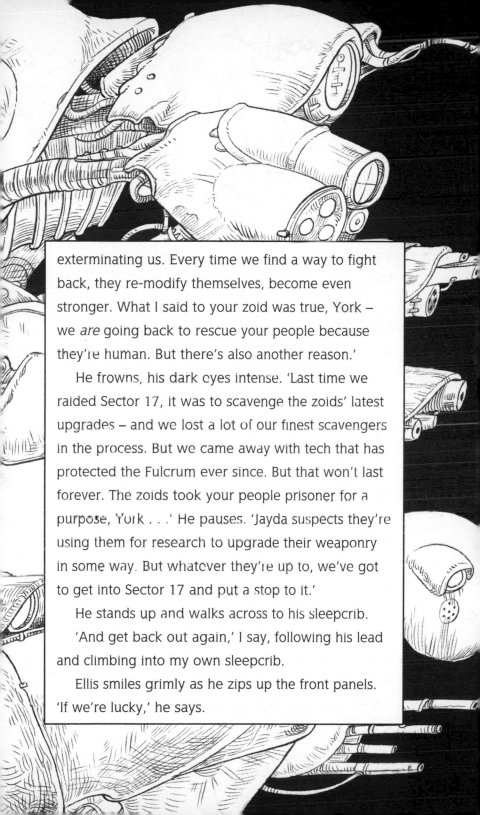

exterminating us. Every time we find a way to fight back, they re-modify themselves, become even stronger. What I said to your zoid was true, York – we *are* going back to rescue your people because they're human. But there's also another reason.'

He frowns, his dark eyes intense. 'Last time we raided Sector 17, it was to scavenge the zoids' latest upgrades – and we lost a lot of our finest scavengers in the process. But we came away with tech that has protected the Fulcrum ever since. But that won't last forever. The zoids took your people prisoner for a purpose, York . . .' He pauses. 'Jayda suspects they're using them for research to upgrade their weaponry in some way. But whatever they're up to, we've got to get into Sector 17 and put a stop to it.'

He stands up and walks across to his sleepcrib.

'And get back out again,' I say, following his lead and climbing into my own sleepcrib.

Ellis smiles grimly as he zips up the front panels. 'If we're lucky,' he says.

29

Caliph wakes me, licking my cheek. I open my eyes to see his pointy little face in front of me.

'Is it that time already?' I say. I'm not disappointed to have been woken.

I was dreaming that I was inside Sector 17, in the place I saw on the download I got from that killer zoid I zilched. The vast building. The silver-red of the force field penning me in. Lina, Dek and Bronx were there too. A zoid was coming towards me, a strange weapon in its pincers: a weapon that sprouted white fur, and then eight eyes, and then jaws full of visiglass fangs . . .

I glance at my scanner. It's not far

off six. I sit up and crawl out of my sleepcrib.

Ellis is still asleep and snoring. Some of the other scavengers from the Fulcrum are already up though, and all the cyclops look ready for action. Belle is standing looking in the direction of Sector 17, just as she was when I turned in.

'You been standing there all night?' I say.

She shakes her head. 'I have also been sitting,' she says.

I laugh. Sometimes she can be so literal. Then I remember my dream.

The download from the killer zoid.

I find it on my scanner. The vast building. The silver-red of the force field penning my friends in. The steel chairs. Gaffer Jed . . .

It's too painful to watch. I show it to Belle. 'Can you identify the building they're in?' I ask.

She looks, nods, then grasps the scanner and downloads the information into her own memory banks.

'Based on this visual data and reconfigured upload information from Ralph, I calculate that your people are being held in the meta-tertiary upgrade facility,' she tells me. She points to the horizon. 'There.'

I adjust my recon-sight and enlarge the area Belle is indicating. There are two domes, with a mass of pulsing lights criss-crossing in front of them.

A force field of some sort.

Ellis and the rest of the scavengers are up by now, and have gathered round. They all stare off towards Sector 17 and the vast white and silver domes. They exchange grim glances. Someone lets out a low whistle . . .

Ellis looks at his scanner. 'Ten minutes,' he says.

And ten minutes later we depart.

We pass by more of the sump-oil tanks and the pipe-vents, which emit intermittent blasts of hot air that smells of scorched metal. My recon-sight is awash with yellow, green, blue and red heat-sigs, but I can see no zoids. The other scavengers are also puzzled. Then we all realize at once that it's the force field causing this disturbance.

We shut off our recon-sights. And scanners. They're useless to us here. We'll have to enter Sector 17 blind. Ahead of us, the domes get closer . . .

But first we have to get through the force field.

Belle isn't fazed. While the rest of us hunker down behind pipe-vents, checking and loading our weapons, and calming the jittery cyclops, she turns to Ellis.

'The force field is a bio-deflector,' she says. 'It reacts to pulse-signatures and brainwaves. *Living* brainwaves.'

She points to a small visiglass booth beyond the pulsing strands of light that criss-cross the air in front of us. Inside the booth, I can see a glowing holo-panel.

'That's one of the perimeter defence hubs,' Belle

continues. It controls this section of the force field. I can reconfigure the power surges to create a gap large enough for you to enter the sector.'

Through the light strands, I glimpse Sector 17 stretching off into the distance, and the two domes. Around them there are zoids coming and going. Large and small. Gigantic mech-monsters and tiny scuttle-mice, and every size and type of zoid in between. It's hard to identify specific models through the force field's shimmer, but I can make out tanglers, sluicers and welders, as well as strange-looking zoids whose functions are completely unknown to me.

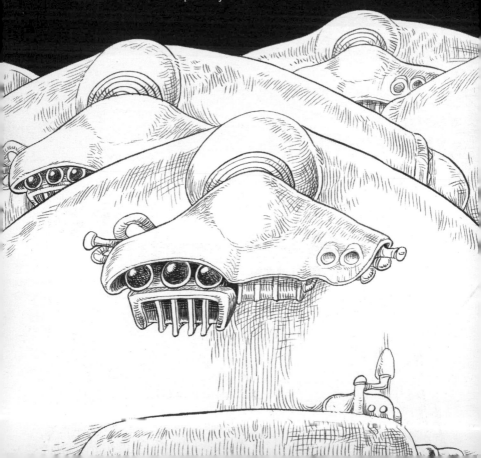

It is a scavenger's paradise – or would be if it wasn't for one thing . . .

Killer zoids.

I spot one. Then another. And another. I can see them through the haze. Inert. Standing in ranks beside the domes. It reminds me of the Robot Hub. Like the ancient robots there, these killer zoids seem to be powered down.

They obviously haven't detected us. Not yet.

'There wasn't a force field when we raided last time,' Ellis says. 'How are you going to get through

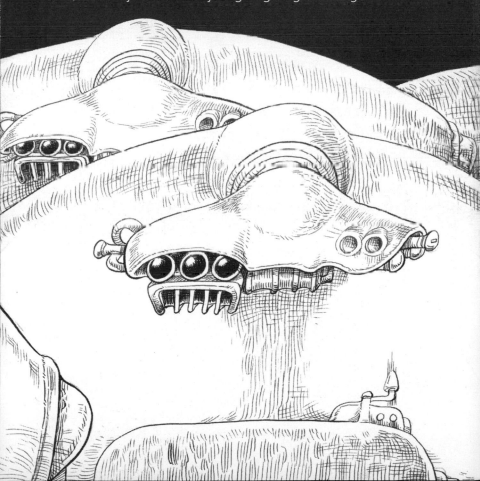

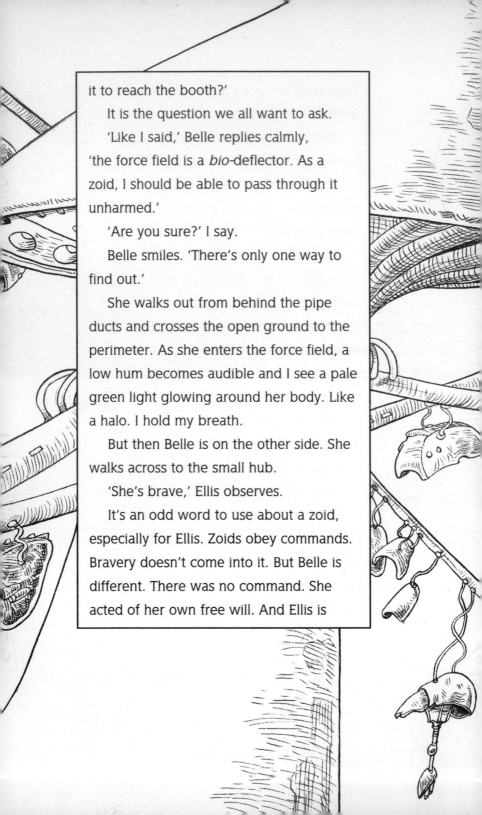

it to reach the booth?'

It is the question we all want to ask.

'Like I said,' Belle replies calmly, 'the force field is a *bio*-deflector. As a zoid, I should be able to pass through it unharmed.'

'Are you sure?' I say.

Belle smiles. 'There's only one way to find out.'

She walks out from behind the pipe ducts and crosses the open ground to the perimeter. As she enters the force field, a low hum becomes audible and I see a pale green light glowing around her body. Like a halo. I hold my breath.

But then Belle is on the other side. She walks across to the small hub.

'She's brave,' Ellis observes.

It's an odd word to use about a zoid, especially for Ellis. Zoids obey commands. Bravery doesn't come into it. But Belle is different. There was no command. She acted of her own free will. And Ellis is

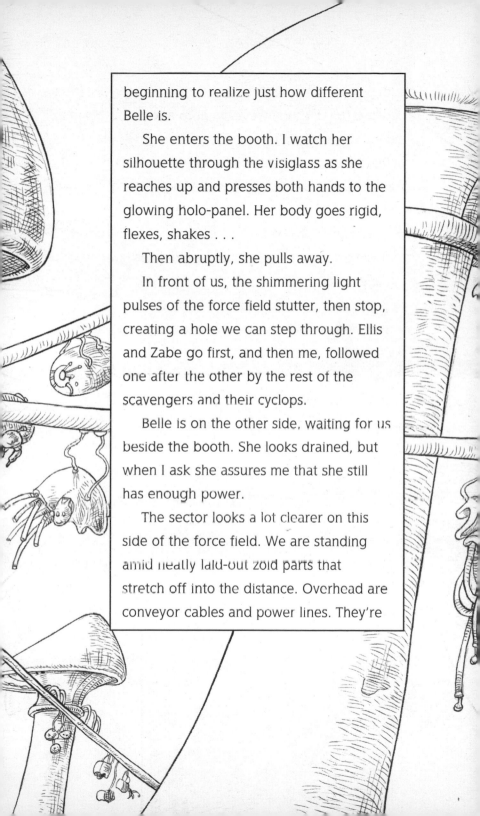

beginning to realize just how different Belle is.

She enters the booth. I watch her silhouette through the visiglass as she reaches up and presses both hands to the glowing holo-panel. Her body goes rigid, flexes, shakes . . .

Then abruptly, she pulls away.

In front of us, the shimmering light pulses of the force field stutter, then stop, creating a hole we can step through. Ellis and Zabe go first, and then me, followed one after the other by the rest of the scavengers and their cyclops.

Belle is on the other side, waiting for us beside the booth. She looks drained, but when I ask she assures me that she still has enough power.

The sector looks a lot clearer on this side of the force field. We are standing amid neatly laid-out zoid parts that stretch off into the distance. Overhead are conveyor cables and power lines. They're

strung out in intricate sequences, spanning the distances
between what look like energy hubs that sprout up like
huge mushrooms. The two domes tower over the entire
sector, white and glistening, with the power lines and
conveyor cables converging in dense clusters at the apex
of each one.

Ellis climbs up onto one of Zabe's shoulders, and Belle
and I climb onto the other, loaded pulsers in our hands.
Silently, around us, the other scavengers mount their
cyclops. All eyes turn to Belle.

Her head is lowered and her eyes stare blankly as she
accesses her memory bank.

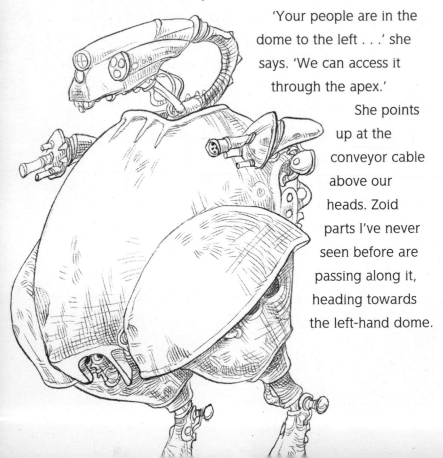

'Your people are in the
dome to the left . . .' she
says. 'We can access it
through the apex.'

She points
up at the
conveyor cable
above our
heads. Zoid
parts I've never
seen before are
passing along it,
heading towards
the left-hand dome.

Across the vast fields of zoid parts in front of us, zoid workers at ground level are going about their tasks. Without working recon-sights, we can't see their heat-sigs – but then, with our coolant suits and the cyclops' coolant packs, they can't see ours either. If we get too close though, then their vision sensors will tell them that we're no zoids.

We're going to have to be careful. And quick. It's just as well we've got the cyclops.

Zabe leaps up and grasps the moving conveyor cable and holds on tight. We're whisked high overhead. Around us, the air is filled with silently leaping cyclops and their riders.

The conveyor cable rises higher. It takes us swiftly towards the apex of the dome in the distance, across what is now a patchwork of zoid parts spread out below our feet. The top of the dome comes nearer, and I shudder as I see we're now passing directly over rank after rank of killer zoids.

Luckily, like I said, they're powered down. And the maintenance zoids scurrying around them don't look up.

Then I feel Belle tense beside me.

At the top of the dome is a loading platform. There a maintenance zoid is taking the zoid parts from the conveyor cable and sorting them into chutes that lead down into the interior of the dome. Any moment now, its angular head is going to swivel round and its vision sensor is going to see a line of shaggy blue critters and scavengers coming towards it.

All at once, Belle leaps from Zabe's shoulder and sails through the air. She lands on top of the maintenance zoid. I see a flash of metal as her cutter severs the zoid's neck cables – just as we saw Ellis do in the tube-forest. By the time Zabe, Ellis and I reach the loading platform and drop from the cable, Belle has deactivated the zoid. She staggers back.

'You need to recharge,' I tell her.

The others are arriving and the platform is filling up.

'No time,' Belle says. 'Look . . .'

I peer down through the opening at the apex of the dome. Below me is the inside of a vast building I have seen before – the holding pen with the glowing electro-mesh on one side and steel chairs ringed by an array of tools on the other. The chutes carrying zoid parts descend from the loading platform, down through the floor of the dome below and into what must be underground zoid production lines.

I can see people huddled together behind the electro-mesh. My people. Though in the low light inside the dome, I can't make out their faces.

On the far side of the mesh, zoids are moving about on thin, curved, tripod legs, clicking and buzzing as they communicate with each other. They're some sort of engineer zoids – the first I've ever seen – and as I watch, they sort through the evil-looking tools arrayed around the steel chairs, while projecting holo-images into mid-air from lenses in their round bodies.

The air in the dome below is warm and rank, but I shudder when I see the images. They are schematics

of human brains. Frontal lobe. Cerebellum. Neural pathways.

These zoids are trying to map the human mind, and they're using live humans to do it.

I'm nudged and jostled as the scavengers around me take out their cutters.

'Quick and clean,' whispers Ellis. 'And no noise.'

The scavengers nod. They were trained for moments like this. So was I. I take out my own cutter.

Ellis turns to Belle. 'Can you deactivate the electro-mesh?'

Belle nods slowly, but doesn't speak. I only hope she has enough power left.

'I'll watch your back,' I tell her.

We attach zip cords to the packs worn by the cyclops, and when Ellis gives the signal we drop down into the dome without a sound. Belle and I land on a zoid, and I slash down with my cutter, while around me forty other scavengers do the same.

We outnumber them two to one, and they don't know what's hit them. The zoids go down, zoid-juice spurting from severed limbs and head parts.

My zoid crashes to the floor. I rip out its neck cables then slice down through its core. The holo-image it's projecting – a human skull – shimmers, then blinks off.

I swing back on my zip cord, release it and land on

the floor. Belle lands beside me and stumbles. I catch her before she falls.

'The electro-mesh,' she says tonelessly and approaches the side of the dome closed off by its glowing red strands. Behind the mesh, frightened faces stare back at me.

Faces I recognize.

'York? York, is that you?'

It's Lina. And beside her is Dek, thin and ill-looking and minus his cybernetic arm.

'It's all right,' I tell them. 'We'll get you out of there . . .'

I turn to Belle.

She's crouched down, prising the cover off the mesh control unit embedded in the floor. As I watch, she reaches inside.

An arc of blue-white light shoots out from the unit and up her arm. Her body trembles. Her synth-skin glows and I can see vein-like tubes pulsing beneath the surface.

The electro-mesh fizzes, then snaps off.

Belle slumps to the floor. She has drained the last of her power. I turn to the disabled zoid and tear out its energy core, then run to Belle and crouch down beside her.

Lina, Dek and the others have stumbled out of the

holding pen and are looking around at the fallen zoids and the unfamiliar scavengers. They stare open-mouthed as, from the opening above, the huge shaggy blue cyclops swing down to join them.

I press the energy core I've ripped out of the zoid to

Belle's chest and feel the heat as its power is transferred. She gasps as she recharges in one massive jolt. Then sits up. I realize my hands are burning and let go of the white-hot energy core, which drops to the floor.

'Who is she?' Lina is staring down at Belle, whose power plate is glowing from beneath her flakcoat. '*What* is she?'

I ignore the question as I blow on my rapidly blistering fingers. When I look up, Lina is staring at me, her eyes filled with tears.

'It's . . . it's been awful . . .' she begins, before sobs cut her short.

'We've been here five days, York – we thought you weren't coming,' says Dek.

'Six, isn't it?' says Lina.

'Seven,' I say quietly.

Dek shakes his head in disbelief. 'As long as that? They've been feeding us our own proto-mix,' he says. 'Keeping us alive so they can study us,' he adds bitterly.

'Then they take us away . . . one by one . . .' Lina wails.

'Oldest first,' says Dek, nodding.

'They took my grandpa first,' Lina whispers tearfully. 'Then Fenda, and Mercer . . . Deal, Callow, Finn . . .'

'And Bronx,' says Dek.

I feel numb. 'Bronx?' I repeat.

'To the other dome,' says Dek. 'Just before you got here.'

Belle is back on her feet. The Fulcrum scavengers have gathered the rest of the Inposters together in the centre of the dome and are busy setting explosives around the walls.

Ellis approaches. 'It's about to get noisy round here. But before this place goes up and the shooting starts,' he says, looking at Belle and me, 'we'd better find this Bronx of yours.'

I turn to Lina and Dek. 'Go with the others,' I say. 'They'll look after you.'

The scavengers from the Fulcrum have finished setting the demolition charges around the dome, and their cyclops are fully laden with the other Inpost survivors.

'Get to the gap in the perimeter fence,' Ellis instructs Garvey and Muldoon. 'And wait for us there.'

'We've set the detonators to go off in one hour. Will that be long enough?' Garvey asks.

'It'll have to be,' says Ellis.

Lina grabs my arm. 'But you, York,' she protests. Her gaze flits between my face and Belle's. 'What about *you?*'

I take her hands in mine. Look into her eyes. 'I have to find Bronx,' I tell her.

'And my grandpa?' she says, her voice tremulous.

'Gaffer Jed too,' I say. 'Go,' I tell her, gently but firmly. 'Go now.'

'Come on, Lina,' says Dek.

He pulls her away from me, and I'm grateful to him.

They head after the others. Lina looks back at me
one last time.

   'Be careful,' she mouths.

   I nod, then turn away. The scavengers
fire electro-magnetic zip lines through the
opening at the apex of the dome, and they
and their cyclops rise silently upwards with
their precious cargo.

   We are alone, Ellis, Belle and I,
surrounded by zoid wreckage and gunk.
The low hum of the zoid production
lines rises from below to fill the
silence in the
dome.

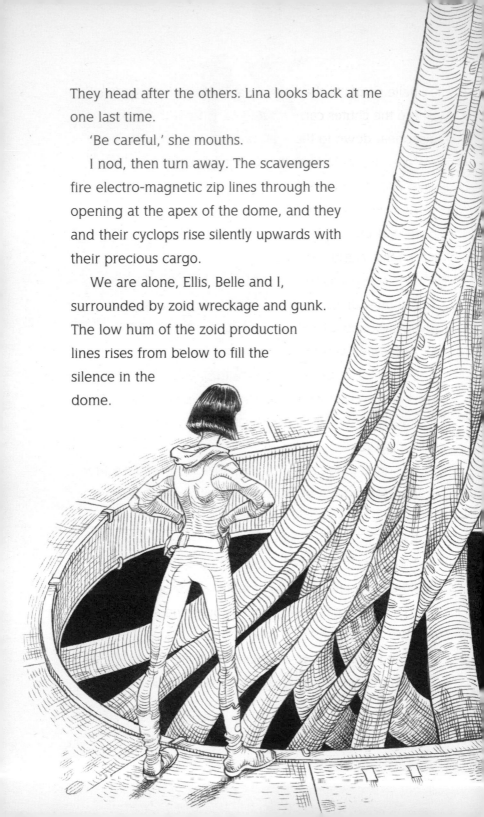

Belle points to the opening at the centre of the floor, where the chutes carrying zoid parts from the apex disappear down to the level below.

'We can get to the other dome through there,' she says, accessing the schematics in her memory banks.

As we head towards it, Caliph suddenly pokes his head up from inside my flakcoat and looks round. I stroke him behind the ears.

'I'd keep my head down if I were you,' I tell him.

Caliph squeaks, almost like he's understood, and dives back down inside.

'This way,' says Belle.

She clings onto the underside of one of the chutes, arms and legs crossed, then slides down into the darkness below. Ellis and I check our coolant suits, then follow her.

It is quite a ride, the smooth metal of the chute a blur in front of my face as I slide down. I hear the explosive percussion of the production lines getting louder, and look down.

The place is vast, extending in all directions further than I can see. It stinks of hot metal and scorched grease. The chutes spiral down through the air and empty their contents onto huge conveyer belts. The low chugging noise they make mixes in with the buzz, clash and din of power-tools. Running alongside the conveyor belts are suspended tracks, with zoids hanging from them in various states of completion. As we slide down towards the floor, I see teams of workzoids swarming round these hanging zoids, welding and wiring components into place in showers of sparks.

Before we reach the conveyor belt, Belle uncrosses her legs and hangs by her arms for a moment. Then she lets go and drops into a narrow channel in the floor directly below.

Ellis and I do the same. As I land, I find myself knee-deep in twists of metal filings and wire offcuts from the production line just above our heads.

'This waste channel will take us to the central sump directly beneath the second dome,' Belle tells us.

Ellis smiles. He is finding out how useful a companion Belle can be.

'But watch out for the recycling zoids,' Belle warns us.

Ellis pauses, the smile fading from his face. Without recon-sights, we're going to have to rely on our own eyes and quick reflexes, we both realize.

Ellis reaches into his backcan and pulls out a couple of gunkballs, their detonator charges primed. He presses them against the wall of the waste channel and sets the timer.

'Let's go,' he says.

Belle leads the way along the channel. We crawl on hands and knees through the scraps of metal and wire, while above us the workzoids go about their tasks in a deafening cacophony. Sparks and glowing metal shavings rain down on us. I glance up. Just above me, on the production line, a newly constructed zoid hangs from the suspended track. It is as broad as it is tall, clad in angular panels of armour that cover every movable joint. And it's armed. Every last square centimetre of the zoid bristles with weaponry. Lasers. Grenade launchers. Surge-lances. Power-nets . . .

It's a killer zoid, but like no killer zoid I've ever seen. This must be the very latest upgrade.

It's being checked over by two workzoids. They're configuring the weapons system and realigning the target sights. I guess that, when their checks are complete, this zoid will join the ranks of the killer zoids I saw outside.

Ellis looks at me, his expression grim. 'A whole new army,' he whispers, as he presses three gunkballs into the wall of the waste channel directly beneath the workstation.

Suddenly, out of the shadows in front of us, a zoid scuttles forward, nozzles on either side of its body sucking up the wire and metal debris. As it approaches, its three visual sensors swivel in its head and glow red.

Belle reacts in an instant. Her arm lunges forward, she seizes the zoid by one nozzle and slams its body against the wall, flattening its head into a mush of circuitry and zoid-juice. Above us in the din of the production lines, the worker-zoids carry out their checks, unaware of what's just happened.

We leave the fizzing wreckage of the recycling zoids behind us and continue along the waste channel. Sweat drips down my face, stinging my eyes. My knees are sore. My back aches, and I wish I could stand up straight and stretch. But now she's recharged, Belle is tireless.

At last she leads us out of the cramped channel and into an immense circular chamber full of thick, intertwined cables that lead up towards a black vaulted ceiling high above. Without pausing, Belle begins to

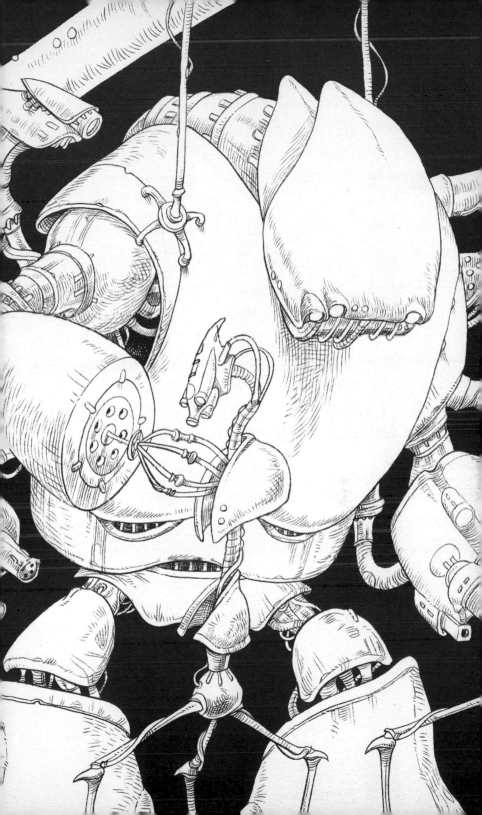

climb and, having laid the last of his gunkball explosives, so does Ellis.

We must be directly beneath the second dome, I realize. Somewhere above us is Bronx. I take a deep breath and, muscles protesting, begin to climb.

At the top, Belle uses a heat-pick to release the bolts on an access hatch and carefully pushes the metal cover to one side. In the circle of black above, I can see constellations of twinkling lights. A low babble of voices fills the air. I can't make out a single word, but the weird jabbering sound gives me the creeps.

Belle pushes her head up through the opening. Ellis and I climb up beside her and look up into the dome. I clamp a hand over my mouth, unable to believe what I see.

The air is warm and sickly sweet and throbs with the sound of the low, muttering voices. The walls are lined with a web of flickering light tracks, pulsing with energy.

At the centre of the dome, suspended from glowing neuro-lines, are mind-tombs. Hundreds of them. Dark and inactive. They are what is left of the Half-Lifes the zoids have taken from the human settlements that they have destroyed down the centuries. Five hundred years of destruction . . .

And then I see it. A mega-zoid hanging in mid-air at the centre of the suspended mind-tombs.

'Hot swarf!' I gasp.

Eight tentacle-like pipes stick out from the zoid's shimmering metal head and are attached to the mind-tombs closest to it. A gigantic black body, smooth and gleaming, hangs down beneath the zoid's head.

This zoid is monstrous – but it's not as monstrous as the object that stands on the floor beneath it . . .

It is a visiglass cube filled with a green plasma gel. And there, looming up from its depths, is a face. A

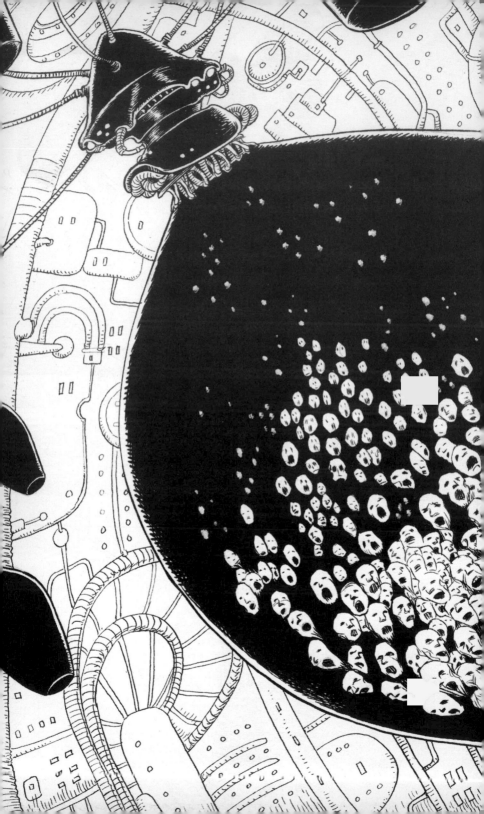

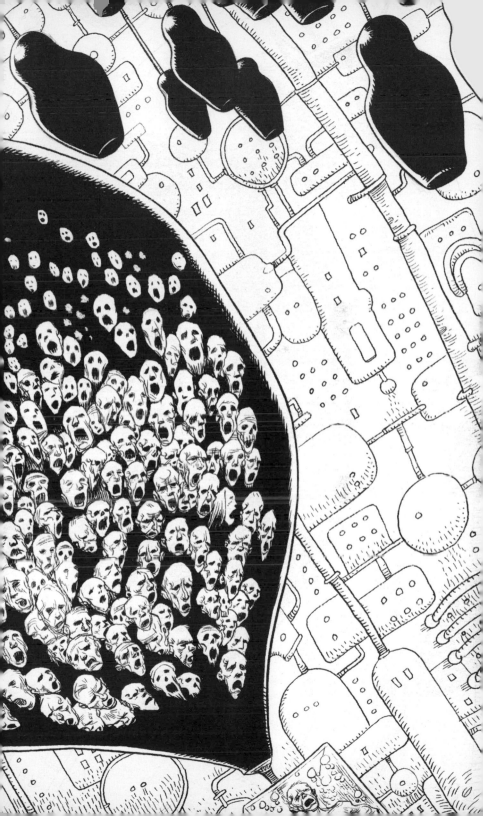

human face. A face that is screaming soundlessly, and that I recognize at once.

Bronx.

I watch in horror as the body of the huge zoid begins to glow. Blotches of light mottle its black surface. They are blurred at first, then grow sharper, increasing in number and overlapping each other until the whole bulbous body is lit up from within.

I see that they are faces. Hundreds of them. Hovering like pale animated masks. They twist and contort, their eyes wild and rolling, their mouths grimacing in torment. Faces of the Half-Lives. Faces from the Inpost. Gaffer Jed. The sound of muttering voices rises to a deafening chorus of human screams.

Beside me, I hear Ellis groan. I turn to him. His face is white.

'I'd hoped they were just rumours,' he's muttering. 'I'd prayed it couldn't be true . . .'

'What *is* it?' I whisper.

Ellis shakes his head, his gaze fixed on the hideous creature. 'It's the death zoid.'

'Death zoid,' I repeat, the words chilling me to my core.

Then the zoid starts moving.

It lowers its glowing body until the tip touches the surface of the green plasma gel. The gel instantly churns and crackles with synaptic energy, and I see Bronx's body convulse into spasms. Flashes of light surge up from his head, through the gel and into the zoid's body.

Much more of this and Bronx's mind will be swallowed up and imprisoned within the zoid along with the others. Downloaded.

'*Enough!*'

It is Ellis. His voice rises above the screams as he leaps from the hatch and races across the floor of the dome. I'm up and on my feet too. So is Belle.

Ellis leaps into the air, grabs hold of a neuro-line and pulls himself up onto a hanging mind-tomb. Belle and I dash towards the plasma-gel cube. Belle throws me the heat-pick and I use it to attack the side of the cube. The visiglass cracks. Belle arches her back and kicks the cube once . . . twice . . . three times . . .

Suddenly the visiglass shatters and the plasma gel comes pouring out onto the floor – and with it Bronx, who flops heavily onto his back.

I crouch down. Clear the gel from his nostrils, his mouth. His eyes are open, but they're staring blindly.

'Bronx,' I whisper, as I roll him over onto his side. 'Bronx . . . Bronx . . .'

There's no pulse. I press down on his chest. Again and again, the heel of my hand forcing his ribs down and up. He can't be dead. He can't be. Not Bronx. He's been

there for me all my life – the leader of the Inpost. My
mentor. My friend . . .

'York, look out!' Belle shouts.

But I'm dazed. In shock. I feel Belle's grip on my arm
and a sharp tug as she pulls me away. I topple over onto
my back and find myself staring upward.

Above me, Ellis is swinging from one data-tower
to the next. His weight snaps one of the neuro-lines.
A data-tower comes crashing to the ground. It misses
me by millimetres and ends up lying shattered next
to Bronx's lifeless body. Ellis leaps from another of
the black data-
towers onto the
shimmering metal
head of the
zoid.

The screams are louder than ever.

Ellis is a scavenger, born and bred. Just like me. He has spotted the zoid's weak spot and is going for it.

The cutter he's holding flashes as he plunges his hand into the head of the zoid, sending globules of zoid-juice spurting out into the air.

The zoid bucks and writhes, tearing its tentacles from their anchor points in the surrounding mind-tombs – three, four, five, six – until the monstrous zoid is held up by only two of its eight tentacle-pipes. As they whiplash free, I see that the pipes are tipped with razor-sharp neuro-spikes.

Ellis is clinging onto the zoid's head, cutting deep down into its cerebral core. The human screams from the zoid's body are deafening. And the faces of the Half-Lifes – each with their consciousness trapped within – are glowing red. With horror I glimpse Bronx's face among them. And so does Belle. She dashes forward, reaches up and presses a hand against the surface.

Then everything happens at once.

Ellis rips his arm free of the zoid's head in triumph, a dripping urilium cortex in his hand. The next moment I see a spurt of blood as a vicious neuro-spike bursts through his chest. He grimaces and his body shudders as five more of the neuro-spikes skewer his body.

The zoid freezes. Its body goes black. The screams

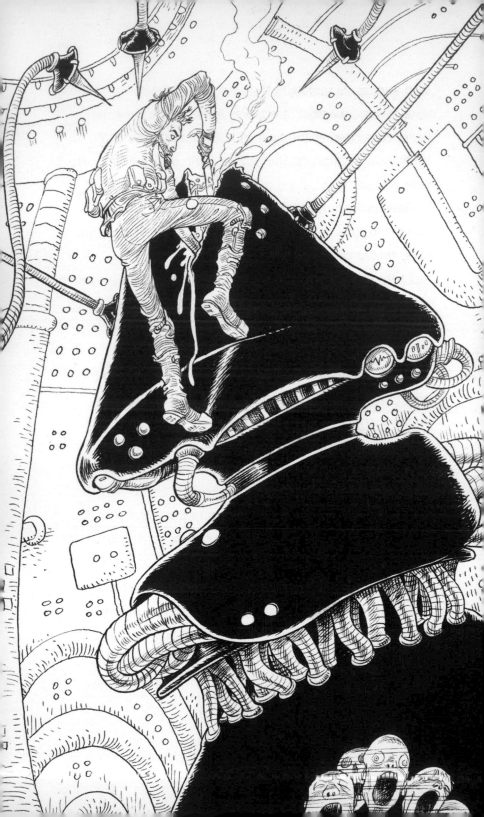

stop and, as its remaining two tentacles detach from the data-towers, the zoid falls to the floor. Ellis falls with it. Belle leaps clear as the head shatters and the now dull body disintegrates, splattering the walls of the dome with zoid-juice.

Belle picks herself up. She walks over to me, bends down and runs her hand down my cheek. 'York,' she says, 'we've got to get out of here.'

I try to clear my head. 'Ellis?' I whisper.

He is lying on his side a little way off, the neuro-spikes still embedded in his back and chest. He is dead.

I shake my head miserably. First Bronx. Now Ellis . . .

Belle takes my hand and helps me to my feet. Then, pulling me close to her, she fires a zip line up at an opening at the apex of the dome.

The walls are glowing brightly now, the light tracks turning a deep, pulsating red. An alarm has been triggered.

Belle activates the line and we sail up through the air. When we reach the top, we pull ourselves out onto the smooth curved roof of the dome. Below us, I can see ranks of killer zoids. Hundreds of them. Weapons systems begin to whirr as they power up. Heads rise on cabled necks as their visual sensors start to glow.

The first killer zoid straightens up and takes a step forward.

Suddenly we see a familiar figure. It's Ellis's cyclops, Zabe, hunkered down and waiting patiently on the loading platform at the top of the first dome. The others have left and will be waiting for us at the perimeter.

As soon as he catches sight of us, Zabe clambers to his feet and jumps from the platform onto the curved side of the dome. He slides down the smooth surface, gathering speed as the slope increases until he free-falls . . .
and hits the ground, his powerful arms cushioning his landing.

The first rank of killer zoids have powered up now. Below us I see a ripple of red as the ranks behind stir into life. Weapons systems whirr and click, visual sensors glow, heads turn to scan the surroundings.

Down on the ground, Zabe gallops across the open space between the domes towards us. When he reaches the dome we're standing on, he begins to climb. His claws dig into the smooth surface as he pulls himself up.

On the ground the killer zoids are advancing from all sides in glistening ranks. I hear the ominous whine of pulsers locking on to their targets.

Zabe reaches us. We scramble onto his shoulders as the first volley of laser fire explodes around us. With our coolant suits on, the zoids are relying on their visual sensors. But now they've got our range the next volley will be fatal.

I hear the whine and . . .

There is a blinding flash. An ear splitting noise. The shock wave hits us.

Zabe leaps into the air.

The first dome has exploded. An immense fireball goes up. Smoke and glowing debris spiral out from its molten centre.

The ground quakes and the killer zoids stagger this way and that, fighting to regain their balance.

Zabe lands on top of one of the bulbous energy hubs

that cover Sector 17. Conveyor cables sprout out from it in all directions. He grabs hold of one and swings off along it, heading for the perimeter force field, which we can see shimmering in the distance.

There is another explosion. And another. A whole series of blasts deep below the ground. The gunkballs that Ellis set in the zoid production lines are going off.

I look back.

The first dome is in ruins. Black smoke from the underground production lines is billowing from the second dome. Exit hatches have burst open and a stream of workzoids – blackened, limbs blown off, sensors flashing – are pouring out. They stumble. They totter. They go in circles, colliding with the killer zoids, who are attempting to regroup.

I realize that without the monstrous death zoid that Ellis destroyed, they lack a central brain to tell them what to do. But it won't last long. Already, engineer zoids on thin tripod legs are moving among the ranks of the killer zoids, their memory

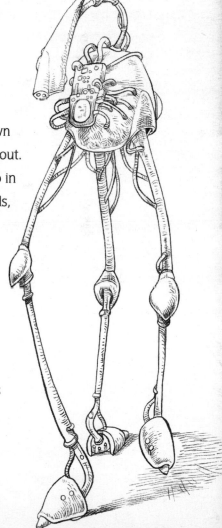

239

banks glowing red within their chests as they download commands.

Sector 17 is damaged. But these zoids are already adapting. We've got to get out of here fast . . .

Hand over hand, Zabe gathers speed as he swings along the cable, over the confused scrum of zoids and on across the fields of zoid parts. When we arrive at the perimeter force field, the Inposters, together with all but two of the scavengers, have made their way through the hole. Garvey and Muldoon are surrounded by the troop of cyclops. The two scavengers greet us as Zabe drops down from the cable.

'Ellis?' says Garvey.

I shake my head. Behind me, Zabe lets out a soft, mournful cry. He seems to understand what has happened.

Muldoon and Garvey exchange glances.

'Join the others,' says Garvey. 'Your zoid must get everyone back to the Fulcrum by any route possible. Can it do that?' he asks.

'*She!*' I snap. 'Her name is Belle.'

Garvey frowns. 'Whatever,' he says. 'Just get a move on.'

Belle steps forward, seemingly unaware of our disagreement. She nods. 'I have the schematics in my memory banks.'

Muldoon shakes his head. 'Who'd have thought it? A zoid leading humans to safety.' He smiles. 'Thank you, Belle.'

'*Go*,' says Garvey urgently. 'We'll buy you as much time as we can—'

'You'd do that for us?' I say.

'It's what Ellis would have wanted.'

I turn and follow Belle through the hole in the force field. Zabe stays behind. He looks lost and bewildered without his master.

A small body stirs, warm against my chest. Caliph, loyal and trusting, is still curled up in the inside pocket of my flakcoat. I reach inside and stroke his small furry head. I look up and see Dck, Lina and the rest of the Inposters staring back at me. They are pale, tired, ill – and waiting for me to tell them what to do next.

Without Bronx, it seems that they see me as their leader.

Alongside them, the rest of the scavengers from the Fulcrum have powered up their weapons, reset their scanners and recon-sights and are ready to move. They're looking at me too. I look at Belle.

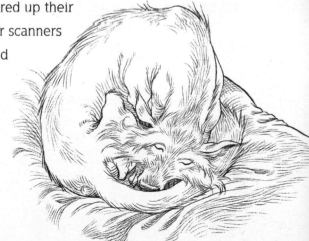

'Get us out of here,' I say.

We set off through the sump reserves. Belle leads the way, running at a pace that tests the weaker members of our group. The scavengers fall back. They help the slower ones and cover our backs as we weave in and out between the circular tanks of black oil.

We haven't gone far when I have to call out for Belle to slow down.

We're getting strung out and risk losing contact with each other. Belle ducks down behind a tank. I join her. As Inposters gather around us, panting and blowing, I see Lina.

She's looking at Belle with a mixture of fascination and awe. Beside her, Dek is struggling. His face is grey and he's gasping to catch his breath.

Laser fire breaks out behind us, vivid flashes of white and yellow and

orange, followed by the crack of explosions. I stare back at the perimeter. The cyclops are swinging along the conveyor cables, speeding away from us across the fields of zoid parts.

The killer zoids are in pursuit. And as I watch they pick off cyclops after cyclops – but not before some of the creatures have dropped down onto their pursuers and attacked them with their long curved claws. Zoids topple to the ground as the claws slash through cables, severing limbs and head units. They crash into the neat rows of zoid parts, scattering them in all directions.

But the killer zoids keep coming. More and more of them.

Garvey and Muldoon are doing their best to lure the zoids away from us, raining down a devastating fire of grenades and gunkballs and laser blasts on their pursuers. They're doing a good job. But not good enough. A phalanx of killer zoids breaks off the chase. They turn back towards the perimeter and head this way.

'We've got to keep moving!' I tell the others as I get to my feet.

We set off at a run again. Belle is up front, leading us towards the grid-plate sector in the distance. The scavengers form a firing line behind us, using the sump tanks as cover. Peering through their recon-sights, they take aim.

The force field barely flickers as, along its length, killer zoids pass through the perimeter and advance towards us. As they approach, the scavengers release a hail of laser fire. It strikes the zoids. Splinters of light fly off in all directions as the laser bolts are deflected by the killer zoids' urilium armour-plating.

The killer zoids open fire and sump tanks explode into burning torches. They're directing their fire over our heads, hitting tanks ahead of us, to the sides and behind, until we're trapped inside a ring of fire.

The heat is intense, forcing the Inposters and scavengers to huddle together in a group. I look at Belle. Her face is impassive. I know that she could leap high over the burning tanks and make her escape, but she doesn't. She stays with us.

Lina and Dek look at me.

'What are we going to do, York?' Lina sobs.

This isn't like the raid on the Inpost. The killer zoids are taking no prisoners. Not now. Their zoid

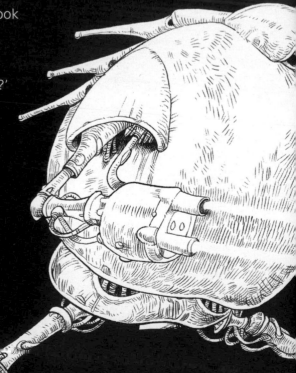

leader is dead and with it whatever warped plan it was
up to. Now the zoids are back to their primary directive.
To exterminate the human race.

Us.

In the distance, the firing in Sector 17 abruptly stops.
It can only mean one thing . . .

Muldoon, Garvey and the brave cyclops have bought us
all the time they could. I only wish that we had made more
use of it. But at least we can die as bravely as they did.

More killer zoids are streaming out of Sector 17 to
join the ones in front of us. Their weapon systems whine
as they lock on.

It's all over.

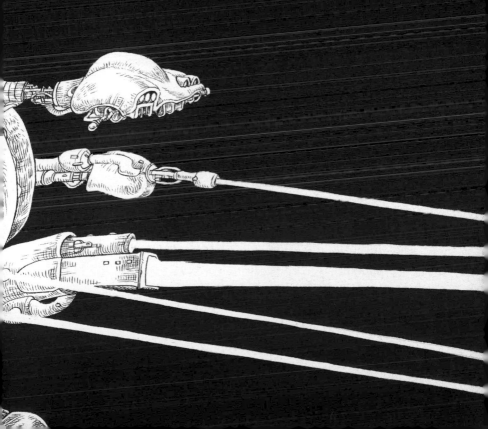

Then I see a flash of white. A wing tip, broad and fine-boned, darts across my vision. I glimpse a head-ridge, a glowing snout . . .

Huge winged critters are swooping down through the air. Glimmermouths. Hundreds of them. They dip low, gathering Inposters and scavengers in their claws and soaring back into the air.

A heavy pall of smoke from the burning sump tanks is blowing across the front ranks of the killer zoids like a curtain. It shields us from their visual units, and the blazing tanks mask us from their heat sensors.

A glimmermouth grasps my shoulders and I feel myself being lifted off the ground. I look up. There's a scar at the top of the left leg. It's *my* glimmermouth. It's come back to rescue me and, judging by the look of things, it has brought the entire flock with it.

It allows me to pull myself up onto its back and we fly up through the blanket of dense smoke, high above the hanging hull lights and into the shadows of the hull structure. Far below, I hear the killer zoids blindly raining

a hailstorm of laser fire onto the sump tanks we have just left.

As we weave in and out of massive hull struts I see the landscape of the Biosphere laid out below me. The grid plates. The pylon forests. The dead havens . . . My world: rusted, overgrown, infested with life that clings to toeholds wherever it can. I'm beginning to realize just how we humans must appear to the zoids – an infestation of parasites in their robot-built world . . .

I look across and see Belle, Lina, Dek and the others held in the claws of slowly flapping glimmermouths. Are they thinking the same as I am? The scavengers I see nod back at me, clearly impressed by the control I seem to have over my glimmermouth as it leads the flock. At the Fulcrum they understand cooperation between humans and critters. With my hands gripping its shoulders, I gently guide the glimmermouth around flux-columns and on through lines of generator towers until I see the dark outline of the convection lakes coming into view. High above them, through the tangle of the tube-forest, I spot the unmistakable pod-clusters of the Fulcrum nestling against the hull structure.

The scavengers see it too, and a cheer goes up, taken up by the Inposters.

Responding to my touch, the glimmermouth swoops down and lands on a broad platform between two of the pods. As the others come in to land, the cyclops in the surrounding nests start up an excited chorus of whoops and cries that bring men, women and children streaming out onto the gantries and viewing platforms all around the Fulcrum to see what's happening.

They soon see that not everyone has returned, and the excitement is mixed with sadness. Wives embrace their husbands. Children cluster round their parents. The scavengers talk of our extraordinary escape and the bravery of Ellis and the other fallen scavengers. I hear my name being repeated over and over in breathless conversations between the scavengers and their loved ones. And I hear Belle's name.

'. . . Belle disabled the force field. Downloaded the schematics of the entire sector . . .'

'We'd never have got into the place, let alone got out again, without Belle . . .'

'Belle protected us humans from her own kind.'

The survivors from the Inpost look dazed but relieved. Lev, Spalding, Tara, Delaware, Fitch, and all the other familiar faces . . . I see them looking wonderingly at the pods, the viewing platforms and the nests of the cyclops tucked between. This settlement is so different from our underground home – a home we know we can never return to. Not now the killer zoids have discovered it. It's no longer safe.

The inhabitants of the Fulcrum welcome the Inposters, help the injured and sick to their infirmary and guide the rest to the refectory in the central pod. Lina goes with Dek, who looks about to collapse. A Fulcrum nurse gently reassures them both as they disappear inside. Belle and I watch them go.

On the pod roofs and gantries all around us, the glimmermouths flex their wings and hoot softly to one another. I turn to my glimmermouth and pat its head.

'Thank you,' I say.

The glimmermouth's red eyes fix on mine and its snout glows. I don't know where these strange creatures have come from, or how they've evolved, but I'm glad we humans share our world with them. Unlike the zoids.

Suddenly the whole flock of glimmermouths takes to the air with hardly a sound – just the soft rustling of the slowly beating wings and their strange haunting calls. My glimmermouth leads them as they wheel in the air and disappear into the depths of the tube-forest.

Everyone else has gone inside the Fulcrum. Belle and I are alone. Then I feel her hand on my arm and look up to see Jayda standing in the doorway. She is staring intently at Belle, then looks at me. Her critter, Gimbel, is sitting on her shoulder, its eight eyes blinking back at us.

'They told me what happened to Ellis,' she says quietly. 'And Garvey and Muldoon.'

'They died bravely,' I say.

Jayda nods. 'They will be missed. But great damage has been done to the zoid cause, York, and your people have been rescued. You and they are welcome to stay here with us . . .' Jayda hesitates, swallows hard then turns her gaze back to Belle. She takes a step forward and reaches out a hand to her. 'As are you,' she says.

35

The Fulcrum is quiet. The central pod has emptied and only Lina and I remain, sitting at one of the refectory tables. Even Caliph is somewhere else, off exploring the nooks and crannies of his new home.

I haven't seen Belle since supper, when she was surrounded by grateful Fulcrum people, who kept pushing food at her that she could not eat. She must be recharging somewhere and I realize that I'm thinking about this zoid girl when a human girl is sitting right in front of me, holding my hand and staring into my eyes.

'This place is wonderful, York,' she's saying. 'Those critters of theirs! And the *food*! I even love being up here in the hull structure, so high above it all . . .'

I smile and feel a pang as I remember the Inpost. And Bronx. I was happy there, and I miss him.

'We can make a new life here,' says Lina, squeezing my hand. 'Can't we, York? . . . York? You haven't heard a word I've said, have you?' She smiles.

'I'm sorry, Lina,' I say. 'It's just that there's so much to take in – and so much has happened since the zoid attack on the Inpost . . .'

'Please, York, I don't want to think about it,' she says, tears welling up. 'That terrible place. My grandpa . . . Can't we just be happy here? Now? Together – you and me?'

She pauses. Looks past me, then wipes her eyes. 'Of course, if you'd rather be with *that*,' she says.

I turn. Belle has entered the refectory pod. She's standing over by the black mind-tomb.

It is not working. The Half-Life within it faded away completely while we were in Sector 17. The people of the Fulcrum don't mention it. According to Jayda the mood was downcast and sombre, with everyone mourning the loss of their Half-Life, even though it hadn't spoken for years. But all that has changed now we're back.

The atmosphere is joyful, full of celebration – despite

the deaths of Ellis and the others. They died for the common good. What's more, their sacrifice will not be in vain. Everyone senses that, with the addition of the Inposters, this is a new beginning for the Fulcrum.

'Belle,' I tell Lina softly. I can't be angry. 'Her name is Belle.'

Lina frowns. 'Listen to yourself, York. It's a machine. A zoid . . .' She looks down at the tabletop to avoid eye contact with Belle. 'And you saw what the zoids did to us,' she whispers. 'To my grandpa. To Bronx . . .'

At the sound of Bronx's name Belle steps forward. 'York,' she says. 'There's something I must show you . . .'

I'm about to get to my feet when Lina beats me to it. She jumps up and bangs her fist on the table. 'Go to your zoid, York!' she says bitterly. 'See if I care!'

And she storms out.

Belle is looking at me quizzically. 'Why has your face gone red?' she asks me.

I ignore her, and feel my face redden even more. 'What did you want to show me?' I say.

Belle turns to the mind-tomb and presses a hand to its smooth black surface. And as I watch, her synth-skin glows and pulses of energy ripple down her arm and into it.

She's downloading from her memory banks.

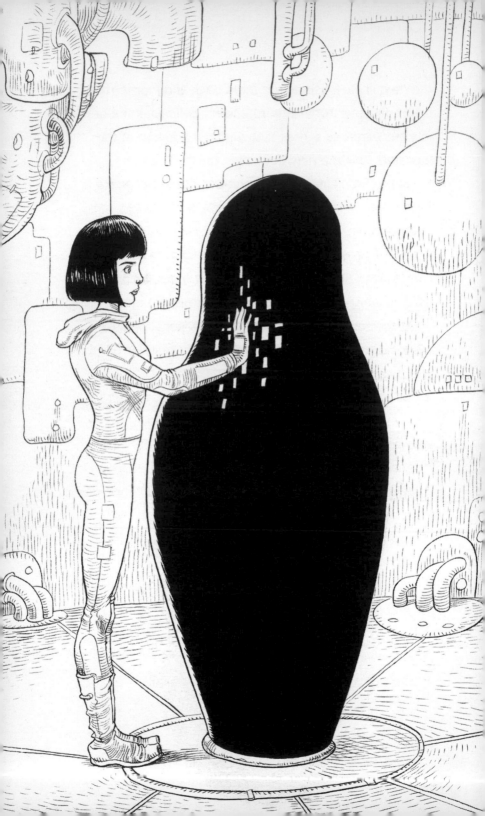

When she's finished, she steps back and turns to me. 'I retrieved this from the zoid leader,' Belle says. 'Before Ellis destroyed it . . .'

'*York? York, is that you?*'

I stare past Belle at the data-tower. It has become a mind-tomb. Glowing beneath its surface is a face.

Bronx's face.

'*Where am I? What happened?*' the glowing face says. '*The last thing I remember is being dragged off by the zoids and dunked in a great vat of plasma gel . . .*'

'Bronx!' I say, rushing up to the mind tomb and bringing my face close to its surface. 'We tried to save you. But we were too late. Your consciousness was uploaded.'

'*You mean . . . that's what that was? I thought it was a dream. A nightmare. The screaming voices, the tortured thoughts . . .*'

Bronx's face glows beneath the surface, his expression a mixture of shock and astonishment as he grapples to understand what has happened to him. He's a bio-tech expert – the best the Inpost had ever known – and it doesn't take him long. '*I've become a Half-Life,*' he breathes.

I nod, my feelings a mixture of sadness and joy.

'*What a strange sensation it is,*' Bronx is saying. '*Almost like floating. I feel perfectly fine – and yet I have no sense of my body . . .*'

'Your body died, Bronx,' I say. 'I tried to revive you. Did everything I could. But I couldn't bring you back.' I pause. I look at Belle, then back at Bronx, the Half-Life. 'But *Belle* did . . .'

'*Belle?*' says Bronx. His eyes focus on the girl standing beside me.

'Belle is a zoid,' I tell him. 'She was created by a tech-doc like you. His name was Dale. But she isn't like the zoids we know, Bronx, the ones we scavenged in the tube-forests around the Inpost. Belle's different. She isn't controlled like they are. Dale engineered her to learn and understand emotions, and to make decisions for herself.'

'*A zoid with free will?*' Bronx sounds incredulous. '*But that means this zoid is almost . . .*'

'. . . human,' I say.

I reach out and take Belle by the hand. But Bronx doesn't seem to be listening. His eyes have closed and he appears to be concentrating. I wait. When he finally opens his eyes again and speaks, he sounds calm and measured. There's a new sense of purpose in his voice.

'*I've just been communicating with someone who says he's a friend of yours, York,*' he says. '*Atherton. From the viewing deck. He's promised to help me adjust to being a Half-Life. He says the life of the mind takes some getting used to, but with his help he's sure that I'll be able to use my tech-knowledge to guide and advise the people here at . . . at . . . What's this place called?*'

'The Fulcrum,' I tell him.

'*That's it, the Fulcrum,*' he says, nodding. '*Oh, and York,*' he says, '*Atherton said to remind you of your promise. What did he mean?*'

'Atherton believes that the cause of the zoid rebellion lies deeper inside the Biosphere, below this level. I promised him that once I'd rescued you and the others, that I would do everything I could to find the answer. But I'm not sure where to start . . .'

'*I am.*'

It is Belle. She has a distant look in her eyes, the look

259

she gets when she's accessing data from her memory
banks.

'When I hacked into the encryption code for
the perimeter force field back at Sector 17, I also
downloaded schematics showing locations of portals to
the mid-deck. There is one in the tube-forest below us.'
She looks at me. 'I can take you there, York.'

I reach out and touch the cool smooth surface of the
mind-tomb.

'I'm so glad you're still here, Bronx. I know you'll take
good care of these people,' I tell the glowing face of my
friend. 'But I must go with Belle.'

'Go with her?'
Lina is in the
doorway. She's
obviously come
back to make up
with me, only
to find that I'm
about to head off
with Belle.

'How can
you choose her
over me?' Lina
asks me. 'She's
synth-skin

and circuitry, York. She's not real . . .'

'The dangers Belle and I have faced together were real,' I say. 'The suckerworms we fought were real. The killer zoids we zilched were real . . .' I look at Belle. 'Our friendship is real.'

My expression softens, and I take Lina by the hand and squeeze it gently.

'Please understand, Lina,' I say. 'I have to find out why our world has gone so wrong. And I need Belle to help me.'

I let go of her hand and leave the refectory pod. Belle follows me.

'Stay safe,' I hear Lina call. 'Both of you.'

SCAVENGER
CHAOS
ZONE

PAUL STEWART
CHRIS RIDDELL

WHEN A MASSIVE SPACESHIP SET OUT ON A MISSION TO FIND NEW EARTH, THE ROBOTS ON-BOARD REBELLED. NOW ONLY A FEW HUMANS REMAIN, HUNTED AND AFRAID . . .

But York is not afraid. He is a scavenger on a mission – a mission to fight back. In a world of tropical rainforests and a huge ocean aquarium, where the people, plants and animals are mutating in strange and disturbing ways, nothing and no one are ever as they seem.

With the fate of his people in his hands and the world in chaos, who can York trust?

Muddle Earth

Paul Stewart
& Chris Riddell

Where would you find a perfumed bog filled with pink stinky hogs and exploding gas frogs, a wizard with only one spell, an ogre who cries a lot and a VERY sarcastic budgie?

Joe Jefferson was just an ordinary schoolboy. But something strange happened when he was walking his dog and now he's Joe the Barbarian – summoned to Muddle Earth to wrestle dragons and be very, very brave. Joe doesn't feel much like a warrior hero (he doesn't look much like one either). But evil is stirring – and someone has to save Muddle Earth from the sinister Dr Cuddles . . .